BEING NOAH

BEING NOAH

CHERYL HARDY

WFP
WordFire Press

Being Noah

by Cheryl Hardy

EBook ISBN: 978-1-68057-082-3
Trade Paperback ISBN: 978-1-68057-081-6
Hardcover ISBN: 978-1-68057-083-0

Edited by Angela Johnson
Cover design by Janet McDonald
Cover artwork images by Adobe Stock
Kevin J. Anderson, Art Director
Published by
WordFire Press, LLC
PO Box 1840
Monument CO 80132
Kevin J. Anderson & Rebecca Moesta, Publishers
WordFire Press eBook Edition 2020
WordFire Press Trade Paperback Edition 2020
WordFire Press Hardcover Edition 2020
Printed in the USA
Join our WordFire Press Readers Group for
sneak previews, updates, new projects, and giveaways.
Sign up at wordfirepress.com

FOREWORD

CANDACE NADON

It is easy to forget how complicated childhood is, just how challenging it is to forge an identity and chart a course towards adulthood, especially in opposition to societal, cultural, and familial forces. The difficulties inherent in the maturation of the self are not confined to adolescence, as is often thought. Rather, they are present throughout childhood and are particularly evident in the liminal space where the ten-year-old exists. No longer a little kid, but not yet a teenager or even a tween, a ten-year-old is caught in a space *between*, where the competing desires for closeness with the family and independence from it are tangled in an ever-shifting continuum and where a young person acutely feels the injustice of not being believed and understood for who they are.

Ten-year-old Noah finds himself in just this space when *Being Noah* begins. Noah is in 4th grade at a Denver-area Montessori School. He loves video games and baseball. He's a good student and loves visiting his grandmother in Paonia, on the Western Slope of Colorado, where he gets to spend all day outdoors and play with his grandmother's horses. Noah's twelve-year-old brother, Sean, is on the Autism Spectrum. He's easily agitated by unfamiliar settings and any situation where there is, as Noah tells us, "noise and chaos." Sean has a service dog, a chocolate lab named Ozzie, who goes everywhere with him and helps to calm him.

Noah loves his brother, and like any little brother, helps him and teases him in equal measure. But Sean's developmental disability is also tough for Noah. Because Sean needs special care, Noah often feels Sean gets more attention from their parents, teachers, and friends, and because the manifestations of Sean's disability sometimes lead to outbursts, Noah is often disappointed by the disruption of their family's routine. And Noah wishes *he* could have a puppy all his own, too. But he knows his parents don't have the bandwidth for another animal in the household.

Noah has another struggle, though, one more profound than the heartbreak of feeling neglected by his overworked and stressed parents. Noah has an ability beyond his brother's brilliant mathematical mind and understanding of complex technological systems.

Noah can see things before they happen, leaving his body to watch events unfold in front of him.

He's also able to communicate with animals, like Ozzie, who help him act on his prescience.

The problem isn't Noah's gift, which over and over Noah uses to help people—rather, the problem is that no one, not Sean, not his mother, not even his beloved grandmother, believes him, even when Noah's sight keeps the people he loves from harm. They think Noah's actions to help them are coincidental, and worse, sometimes meddlesome, which makes Noah feel all the more misunderstood.

Being Noah is the story of Noah's journey towards believing in his gift, even when others don't. It is the story of Noah wrestling with loving and resenting his brother. And above all, it is the story of Noah learning that he is exactly who he is supposed to be.

———

I met Margaret Hardy, or Cheryl, as she preferred to be called, in the summer of 2016, her first semester in Western Colorado University's MFA program in Creative Writing. I team-taught the introductory fiction craft class that July with Russell Davis, the then Fiction Concentration Director, and when Cheryl walked into the classroom with her service dog, a sweet Border Collie named Jetta, her presence calmed the first-day anxiety swirling around the room.

Cheryl was quiet, but observant. She was considerably older than the other students in her cohort and had less writing experience, but she persevered, ever-attentive and willing to challenge herself, Jetta always by her side, her talisman and protector. At the end of the two-week residency, Cheryl had already grown as a writer, and the rest of us, learning from her example, had learned about the quiet compassion that makes space for creative risk taking.

I was given the opportunity to advise Cheryl on her thesis, the project that became the novel *Being Noah*. Cheryl wanted to write a story about a boy who was misunderstood, a boy whose path towards growing up included teaching others as much as it included his own journey towards self-knowledge. She wanted to write a story that acknowledged the spiritual world as valid as the visceral one, and I'll admit I was as skeptical as Noah's parents at first, not sure such a book would appeal to young readers, thinking they would find the story difficult to relate to.

How wrong I was.

As Cheryl's book took shape, I found myself captivated by Noah and his world, and as Cheryl continued to send me chapters, I became more and more convinced by Noah's gift—and more and more convinced that this was a story that young readers would not only love, but would understand with the kind of knowing Wordsworth writes of in "Intimations of Immortality"—the "glory and the freshness of a dream" of the world just beyond our own that we ignore to our own detriment.

When I read the final chapters, I turned from my computer screen and cried, feeling as though I'd been privy to Noah *and* Cheryl's journey towards believing in themselves, believing in their gifts, and believing in the stories they had to offer us.

————

Cheryl Hardy lost her battle with cancer and passed away on June 17, 2019 in hospice care in Grand Junction, CO, not long after she finished the final edits for *Being Noah*. She was awarded her degree posthumously in July of 2019, with her daughter and granddaughter in attendance at the graduation ceremony. Her granddaughter, who is named after her grandmother, read a portion of *Being Noah* earlier that day during the graduating student thesis readings. As her granddaughter read the final chapter of *Being Noah* to a rapt audience of Western faculty, students, and the students' family and friends, I felt the power in Cheryl's words yet again.

It was Cheryl's hope to have *Being Noah* published, and I am sorry she is not able to hold a copy in her own hands. I hope that she knows that her book will reach young people and adults alike. I hope she knows that *Being Noah* is a book for all of us who find ourselves between knowing and not knowing and between doubting ourselves and believing in ourselves. *Being Noah* is a book about understanding that we are already who we need to be, the message Cheryl shared with all who knew her, the same message she lived every day.

CHAPTER ONE

ONE SATURDAY MORNING IN MARCH, the wind began to whistle around the windows and doors. I looked out the living room window and saw the sky had turned black with fast moving clouds. Streaks of lightning followed by booming thunder shook the house a little. Rain started falling in great sheets. Sean and I jumped up off the floor and looked at Mom who was standing in the kitchen. She was watching a cooking show on the small television on the counter and assembling stuff for baking. We all were startled when we heard a loud pop, which sent the room into darkness.

Only moments ago, the sky had been clear with just a few white clouds, normal for spring. My older brother Sean, who is twelve, and I were in the living room, playing the *Need for CandaceSpeed* video game on the television screen. I'm only ten, but I'm a good driver. At least on video games. He didn't stand a chance, I thought. He was trying to crash my green 1969 GTO with his purple 1971 Challenger.

"Arrgh!" he cried out as I twisted my car in front of his, cutting off his attempt to get ahead of me.

Our game vanished with the electricity.

I felt myself pop out of my body, somehow. I can't explain it but when this happens, I see things in my mind that haven't happened yet. I "saw" a huge limb come crashing down off the big elm tree along our driveway. It fell across the concrete and onto the lawn. In my mind, I screamed.

I dashed into the kitchen, where Mom had begun mixing up something that would soon smell yummy, I knew.

"Mom, what should we do?" I exclaimed, fear in my voice.

"Here—look in the bottom kitchen drawer and pull out the emergency candles," she said as she slammed the baking pan into the oven. Our stove is gas, so she could keep cooking, thank goodness. She searched for matches in an upper cabinet. She keeps things like that up high so we can't reach them. She wants to keep possible danger away from us. Like we don't know how to climb. Duh. Okay, maybe it was important when we were little.

"Noah, get a move on. Get those candles," shouted Mom above the noise of thunder and rain. Branches of trees crashed against the house. I've seen pictures of hurricane winds on the news. This wasn't a hurricane, but I thought the trees must look bent over under water and wind like on the news.

"Mom! A big branch is going to fall from the elm tree and hit the lawn!" I exclaimed.

"The tree is fine. Just get those candles over here so I can light them," she said, sounding nervous.

That's what always happens when I have a vision. No one ever believes me. This vision thing happens from time to time. I don't understand why or how. I never know when one is going to pop in.

Sean was useless, just standing in the living room screaming and flapping his arms. Poor Sean. He has mild autism spectrum disorder and doesn't do well with noise and chaos. Sometimes, he has tantrums. His therapy dog, Ozzie, rubbed against Sean's legs, trying to calm him. Ozzie is a two-year-old chocolate Labrador. Just then, we began to hear sirens, like from a fire truck. The screech hurt Ozzie's ears and he howled, adding to the chaos.

I handed a bunch of short white candles to Mom and ran to a window to see if there was a fire. I didn't see anything burning and it seemed the sirens were actually out on the highway a couple blocks away. Right then, a streak of lightning seemed to strike the elm tree by the driveway and a branch split away, just like I saw it happen in my mind. The tree was sizzling, but not really on fire.

"Mom! The tree was hit by lightning, just like I saw," I screamed.

Too busy to even respond, she ran into the garage to collect a couple of kerosene lanterns we keep for camping trips. While the door between the house and the garage was open, my nose felt twitchy and I noticed the air smelled different.

"Mom, what is that smell?" I asked.

"That is ozone. That happens when there is a storm," she replied as she pulled the lanterns off a shelf.

She placed those in the kitchen and downstairs bathroom and lighted them. Then she rushed to the living room to calm Sean, who stood in front of the television, still screaming. I followed her, wanting to stay near. I was freaking out, too, but Sean always gets all the attention because of his disease. When there's a lot of noise or people around, he says he starts feeling buzzy. Sometimes, he goes to sit in his closet. He says he needs quiet time, and darkness. I turned away so Mom wouldn't see my disappointment. It made me sad to be ignored.

Dad was at work, even though it was Saturday. Mom tried calling him from the phone in the living room, but the landline was out with the electricity. My cell phone was in the back pocket of my jeans. I pulled it out and turned it on. It still worked, so I pressed the button for Dad's work number and handed it to her while she comforted Sean the best she could. He doesn't like to be touched, so hugging was not an option. She kept brushing her hands down along the outside of his body, smoothing his energy field. I wished she would hug *me*.

I heard Mom tell Dad what happened but that we were okay. She told him about the huge broken branch from the elm tree. When she got off my phone, she handed it back to me, saying that Dad was also experiencing the storm at his office downtown but would get home when the roads cleared. My shoulders relaxed with relief that he was okay and would arrive soon.

The storm passed on gales of wind and water. It seemed like a long time had passed, but it was only a little while. The electricity was still off, but we were snug with the candles and lanterns. The semi-darkness was a little spooky, I thought.

CHAPTER TWO

SINCE THE POWER WAS OFF, Sean and I began to play a board game. I was sitting on the blue carpet in our living room with Sean, who had quieted down. We were playing Battleship on the coffee table. I was bored with waiting for my brother to take his turn. I was leaning against the purple couch that my mom, whose name is Juliet, had bought. Everyone calls my mom Juliet, except me and Sean. Why she liked purple, I did not know. I like blue myself. I reached down and patted Ozzie on the head. He had stayed by Sean through all the racket, even when the sirens hurt his ears.

I saw that Sean had his grey eyes focused hard on the board. My mind wandered. I was thinking about how my eyes are blue and wondering what causes things like eye color to be different. I always want to know "why" everything. I don't know why I'm so curious, but that's just how I am. My knees were raised, and I started tapping my right foot. I thought that might distract Sean. Part of my strategy to win.

My brother was still studying the board and my thoughts kept drifting. All of a sudden, I felt like I was not in my body. It was like I was floating above it. This was the second time this happened in one day. I wasn't out of my body, but it seemed like it. It was like I was above myself and I could see myself sitting on the floor. I could see everything around me at the same time.

In my mind, I saw an image of Sean on a battleship, firing weapons and being fired upon. Sean's ship was sunk. Aha! I now knew where Sean was keeping his ship. Now that I saw where he was keeping his ship, I knew that I could win, and I popped back into the real world. It's not like what you see in Harry Potter movies. That stuff is made up. I just feel a small jolt. Sometimes I have pictures in my mind of stuff that other people can't see. Sometimes, I have strange dreams, and sometimes, I can hear animals talking to me. I used to think everyone could see what I see, but that's not what happens. They think I make it up. My brother says I'm weird.

"Sean, take your turn," I said. I couldn't wait to beat his pants off.

"Leave me alone. I'm thinking," he replied.

He thinks about things in a different way from me. Sean is analytical. It all has to make sense to him in a math way. I go with what *feels* like the right thing to do.

Besides seeing things happening before they do I also can hear the thoughts of animals. Sometimes, I talk with them.

While Sean was still thinking, Ozzie gazed at me and in my mind, he said "I wish he would make a move. I'm bored with waiting."

I sent a thought back to him. "Me, too. But that's just how Sean does stuff."

Ozzie rolled his eyes at me and sighed.

I have dreams about things that I know nothing about, too. I don't understand why others don't think the same way I do. Seems like they should.

While Sean kept studying the board, I couldn't resist throwing buttery popcorn kernels at him. Mom had put a big bowl on the floor near the board. Whatever she was baking had begun to smell delicious. She had placed paper towels around the bowl to catch stray pieces.

"Stop that, Noah!" exclaimed Sean as he batted popcorn off his face.

"I got you right on the nose," I laughed with taunting glee. I wanted to pester him while he was trying to think. This was also part of my strategy. I love to pester Sean anyway. Ozzie was sitting at Sean's feet, which were crossed in front of him. I'm kind of jealous because he has a dog of his own.

I've been asking to have my own dog. Not that I need a therapy dog. Just one that would sleep on my bed with me, play ball and Frisbee with me, and be just for me. I think a Golden Retriever would be fun. They are so beautiful. And he would be a water dog, too, so he and Ozzie could play in the river together. So far, my parents have resisted getting me a dog. They tell me they don't want to add more responsibility and chaos to our family. I hope to wear them down.

I knew I could get away with throwing popcorn at him because Mom's attention was focused on something she was doing in the kitchen and the lights were still off. By this time, she had removed a cake pan full of brownies from the oven. I could smell more good cooking, like yummy hamburgers and French fries. She was making lunch.

I glanced toward the kitchen at my slender mom out of the corner of my eye to make sure she didn't see me throw popcorn. She had pulled her long brown hair back into a ponytail. She did that sometimes to keep it out of her eyes while she worked.

Sean yelled, "Noah, it's your turn!"

"C3," I said as I popped back to the moment and fired on the spot; I'd seen his ship in my mind.

"Hit," Sean said confused and frustrated that I'd hit his battleship.

"C4," I said with a smile finally sinking his last ship. Ha-ha, I was so happy I'd won the game.

Sean jumped up, shouting at me, "You cheated!"

He began flapping his arms and twisting his body as he shouted. Ozzie startled. Sometimes, like just then, I use my ability to see things not there to give me an advantage.

I made eye contact with Sean and sent love to him through my eyes. I had figured out how this would work on another day a few months ago when Sean was pitching a fit. I felt sorry that he was having a bad time and I wanted him to know that I love him. I thought if I said anything out loud, he would just get more upset, so I locked eyes with him and thought about love. It worked. He calmed down. So now, even though I felt like jumping for joy because I won, I helped to calm my brother instead. It was hard to do in the same moment I was having jealous feelings about Sean, but I knew it was important. Anyway, Sean was right. Because I had the vision, I knew where to fire. I felt guilty about that, though. Was that cheating?

Mom dropped her flipper on the kitchen floor as she rushed to the fuss. Uh-oh.

"Noah, did you cheat?" she demanded.

While I tried to figure out how to answer that, she took Sean to the bathroom to wash popcorn butter off his face. I don't think it is fair that he gets all the attention because of his disability.

Just then, the electricity flashed back on, making me blink till my eyes got used to the light. Mom came back to the room and started putting out the flames on the candles and lanterns. The video game came back on, but she turned off the Xbox and turned on the television to see if there were any reports from downtown where Dad's office was. A reporter was on the screen, standing on a small island of grass with water gushing by her over the street.

I could now smell food burning in the kitchen. The smoke alarm started screeching and that made Sean even more frantic. Ozzie hightailed it out of the bathroom where he had followed Sean, yipping with pain in his ears because of the high-pitched noise. This seemed worse than the distant siren for him. I ran to open the back door so smoke could get out. Mom rushed to turn off the stove and she threw open a window. We almost ran into each other, trying to get rid of the smoke so the noise would stop.

"Noah, get in the kitchen and sit at the kitchen table while I help Sean," she ordered me. I went.

We would have burned hamburgers for lunch, and it was all my fault. I felt guilty.

Did I cheat? If I know what to do, what's wrong with doing it?

I stood back as Mom took Sean to his room. His room is painted restful shades of green. The color helps him be calm. I saw Ozzie follow them, plunking down on the area rug with a NASCAR scene on it. I knew this was not punishment. Sean needed quiet time. But it makes me mad that my parents ignore *me*. I never say anything, though. How can I complain when Sean is suffering?

I sat in the breakfast nook and waited for Mom. The table always smells like Lemon Pledge. I was thinking of something I could say to her. I didn't think I'd cheated. Was I really cheating?

When she came back to the kitchen, she said. "You know throwing popcorn at your brother to distract him is really cheating."

She didn't know that I saw in my head where Sean was keeping his ship and how that showed me where to fire.

"How could distracting Sean be cheating?" I asked.

"Would you like it if he did the same to you?" she asked.

"No."

"There you have it. It is against the rules to distract another player in any game. It is also rude and disrespectful."

"Yeah. I guess."

"Have you started your homework yet?" Mom asked in a terse voice

"It's only Saturday," I whined. She gave me her "don't start with me" look.

"I looked at your assignment notebook. You have a lot to do in math and science."

"Yeah. Okay."

In science, I learn interesting things about the world, so I like that. I think math is boring. I like words. Those tell you about all things. Math is just numbers.

CHAPTER THREE

I GOT my books out of my room and brought them to the table. I like to sit at the table and be with Mom instead of in my room, even if she is mad. The padded wooden chairs are comfy. The nook is surrounded by windows that are covered with short yellow curtains. I saw that Mom had put a small vase of daffodils in the center of the table. They were beginning to wilt a little bit. I was thinking maybe she wouldn't be so mad at me if I went out to the garden and picked some more. But they'd probably been battered by the rain.

There is a wood floor that runs from the kitchen through the separate dining room. There are brown and yellow braided throw rugs scattered along the way. I love to run and jump on a rug and slide the length of the two rooms. I feel like I'm surfing, which is something I haven't tried yet. I wished I could rug surf now, but I'd been told to *sit*.

I worked on homework for a while, keeping my head down. I wanted to escape her angry gaze. Sometimes I can see a faraway look in her eyes when she thinks no one is looking. I thought she wasn't happy when she had that look. And that worried me. Maybe it was something to do with me. But what? Was I that bad of a kid? I did what I was told, usually. I did my chores.

Sometimes I needed to be reminded, though. Maybe if I didn't pick on Sean so much, she would be happier.

After a while, Mom finished putting lunch together and called us to the table. The burned burgers were nasty. I looked at Sean and crossed my eyes as I chewed a bite. He returned the look.

"Do we have to eat every bite, Mom?" I asked.

"Could we have some 7-Up today with our lunch?" Sean asked.

"I guess so. It doesn't have any caffeine."

We are never allowed to have caffeine. Mom says caffeine is for adults, not kids.

I noticed Mom kept looking away, pretending not to see us as we stuffed ourselves with French fries. At least the fries had not burned. Then she let us have brownies. Yum.

After the burned burger lunch, Mom told me to finish my homework in my room. I picked up my books and went down the hall toward my room, which is painted shades of blue, my favorite color. Along the way, I gazed at family portraits on both sides of the hall. On the left are pictures of my dad's ancestors. All look blond. For some reason, people always look grim in pictures from a hundred years ago. Like they were never happy. On the right side of the hall are pictures of my mom's ancestors. All of them are blond, too, except one, a great-grandmother named Martha. In a group picture of her family, all the people are blond except for her. She looks dark. Once, I asked my mom about her. She said she didn't know about the Native blood.

"She told me her mother's name was Dove and that she was a Ute, but I never learned any more about Dove," she explained.

I always want to know more. I touched the picture and it crashed to the floor, breaking the frame and glass. Uh oh. I heard the crash of a plate from the kitchen.

"What have you done now?" Mom screeched.

"I, uh, I uh, I just touched the picture and it fell," I stuttered. "I'll clean it up."

"You will *not* clean it up. That's all I need today, for you to cut yourself. We'd probably have to go to the doctor to get stitches. Get in your room and stay there!" she shouted.

I kind of stared at her, my mouth open. Mom was really pissed at me now.

"Go!" she demanded, pointing a finger toward my room. I went.

I have collections of Matchbox and Hot Wheels cars on my dark blue bookshelves. On my floor is a rug with a picture from the first Transformers movie. I sat at my desk and played Police Procedures, my favorite game. I want to be a policeman someday and I have a lot of cop stuff. Once, my class took a field trip to the nearby police station. I was amazed to learn all that cops do and how the place looked all serious-like and how it smelled like burnt coffee and stuff. At least, that's how it seemed. I wasn't allowed to drink coffee at home. Mom says there's enough jittering going on in the house already. But I liked the smell. If I had it my way, I'd go to the police station every day. I loved it there, and I felt like I never wanted to leave. But the field trip ended, and we went back to school.

CHAPTER FOUR

I STARTED THINKING about helping the police someday. I popped out of my body and began having a vision. I saw myself at the police substation we had visited on the field trip. I liked the desk sergeant's blue uniform with a patch with her name on it. And her badge. She had long black hair that she pulled back into a bun, and warm brown eyes. I wanted to talk to her. She looked kind of nice, but I saw she was busy, so I studied the Wanted posters on the ugly white walls.

Even though this was a vision, I could still smell burnt coffee. In my mind, I saw a box of donuts on a metal table. I looked over the box with chocolate, strawberry and sprinkled treats. Somehow, I knew I was welcome to them if I felt hungry, though nobody said anything. I didn't feel hungry, but I took a chocolate one anyway just because they looked and smelled yummy. I pretend that when I am eating anything, I am growing taller.

"You sure got a lot of wanted men on these posters," I said to the sergeant as I munched the donut. She nodded, busy with a call. I saw that she was taking down information on a message pad.

I thought the men all looked ugly and mean. They looked like they never took a bath or shaved. Some of them looked drunk. The sergeant smiled to herself but kept saying 'uh huh' and 'okay' into the phone. I was staring at the black and white posters, memorizing faces in case I ever saw one of the men on the street.

Still in my vision, I licked my fingers, then wiped them on my shirt. In my mind. In real life, Mom would give me a stern look for doing that. Then I popped back into my body. One of these days I'll make that vision come true. I'm going to be a police officer. I went into the kitchen where Mom was still cleaning and told her about it.

"That won't happen in real life, Noah," she said.

"Sometimes I see things in my mind that haven't happened yet, but then they do happen," I explained.

"I don't think this will happen," she said. I looked down real quick so she wouldn't see how disappointed I felt.

I heard a sound outside and looked out a window. Dad was home, at last. I watched through the window as Dad parked at the curb because of the fallen tree limb across the driveway. I saw him squish through the soggy grass to the backdoor. When he opened the door, Mom turned around in quick surprise and dropped a spoon on the floor, splattering water. She was still a nervous wreck. But it wasn't my fault this time. Was it?

"Oh, crap," she exclaimed, tears spurting from her eyes.

"Mom, are you okay?" I asked, concerned. I jumped up to help her clean.

Dad came in right then and rushed right through the mudroom to wrap her in his arms. His shoes, socks, and jeans were soaked, and he made puddles on the floor. I went into the kitchen and watched them share a big hug. I started wiping up the water with paper towels.

"Are you okay?" he asked.

"It's been a *day*. What do you think about that tree?" she asked.

"We'll have to remove the whole tree," he said.

"Oh, I hate that. We love that shade in the summer," she said.

"Hi Dad. You're all wet," I said.

"Hi Noah," he said as he ruffled my brown hair, which was a little bit long. It came down over my ears. I want to let it grow out a lot. I'm thinking about donating hair to people who make wigs for children who get cancer and lose their own hair during chemotherapy.

"Where is Sean?" he asked.

"He's in his room, having some quiet time with Ozzie," I said.

Dad and Mom rolled eyes at each other.

"Let's talk about it after dinner," he said.

Dad took off his wet shoes and socks, then went upstairs to change into his jeans. When he got back to the kitchen, they started telling each other all they knew about the effects of the storm. By now, the reporter on the television said electricity was back on across town and the roads were no longer flooded. I went back into my room and played Police Procedures some more. I never get tired of it.

A few hours later, I could smell spicy Mexican food cooking in the kitchen. Mom was making my favorite, tacos. Maybe she was over being mad at me. I went back to sit in the breakfast nook so I could hang out with her.

The kitchen also smelled like yeast. Mom bakes her own bread every week. When it is hot, it is so yummy—soft but also crunchy. I love to melt butter on it. She was so happy when Dad got her a gas oven to make the baking easier.

As I watched Mom, she reached toward the wall that was covered with a tall column of shelves where she kept herbs she liked to experiment with. I guess she was making sure she had everything she needed to make a recipe. I studied how she moved her hands. Her movements always seemed full of grace. When she was young, she studied ballet.

"The food is almost ready. You and Sean need to wash up," she said.

"Okay, Mom. I'll tell him."

During dinner, Mom and Dad talked about his work. It was good to hear them talk about anything except all that happened that day.

"I'm designing a new traffic circle to go on Horizon Drive," he explained.

"I've heard people complaining about those traffic circles," she replied.

"I know, but they are helpful in keeping traffic flowing."

"Why do people complain?" I asked.

"They just don't like changing the old ways things have always been done," Dad responded.

"What's wrong with change?"

"You'll understand when you are older," he replied.

Aw, jeez. Grownups always say that.

CHAPTER FIVE

THE NEXT MORNING, the sound of Dad's chainsaw could be heard all over the neighborhood, as we helped him get that huge fallen limb cut up and removed from the driveway. Really, it was more like half the tree had split away. Mom couldn't get her car out of the garage till it was cleared. My friend Brian, who lived next door, and his dad, Dan, came over to help.

"Hey Dan," shouted Dad as he cut his chainsaw off.

"Hey Ron. We thought we could help," said Dan.

He also brought his chainsaw and soon, both were cutting away. Brian and I started hauling cut branches to Dad's white Dodge Ram truck, still parked on the curb. I'm the shortest so I did more hauling while Sean and Brian tossed stuff into the truck bed. As the truck began to fill, Brian jumped into the bed to arrange branches so more could fit.

I looked at him and for some reason, there was a big red 'C' printed across his chest.

What?

I didn't know why I was suddenly seeing a big red 'C' on him. The rest of the morning, every time I looked at him, there it was. I didn't know what to think about that. It wasn't like it was a design on his striped polo shirt. The 'C' looked like it was on his body. He noticed that I was looking at him strangely.

"What's wrong, Noah?" he asked.

I didn't know what to say. Brian wasn't aware that sometimes I see things that aren't really there. He knew I was somewhat weird because of the way I talked sometimes. I didn't want him to know how truly strange I got. The rest of the morning, I made a point of not staring at him.

We worked hard, but also had fun. I didn't like the uneasy feeling I had about Brian so while I tossed some small branches into the truck, I told a joke.

"Hey Brian. Do you know how to bake toilet paper?"

"No, but I can brown it on one side," he responded. We laughed.

"Aw, Noah, that's such an old joke," Sean said with scorn in his voice as he flung a branch on the truck.

We had told this joke to each other many times, but it still got us laughing.

"Okay, Sean. You tell a new one," I said.

"Why do hummingbirds hum?" he asked.

"I don't know," I responded as I tossed a smaller branch.

"Because they don't know the words," he said, laughing. "Now your turn, Brian."

"Okay. Knock, knock," he said.

"Who's there?" asked Sean

"I am."

"I am who?"

"You don't know who you are?" asked Brian.

We were all laughing, even the men, as we kept coming up with knock knock jokes.

Soon, the truck was loaded. Dad moved it further down the curb, and Brian's dad pulled his own red truck to the spot on the curb. We filled that one with branches and smaller chunks of the trunk of the big old tree as the men cut it down. Dad said we would have to get a professional to remove most of the trunk and the stump. I felt sad to see it go. I think we all did.

We were down to twigs, so I grabbed the water hose to wash down the driveway. As I splashed, the water felt cool, so I sprayed it over my sweaty head and face.

"Hey, I want a turn," said Sean.

He sprayed his own head, then Brian took a turn. I grabbed the hose back and sprayed Dad. "Uh-oh." But he was laughing.

We piled into my dad's truck for the trip to the landfill. Brian's dad followed in his truck. After we emptied the trash, we were hot and sweaty and hungry. We rode with Brian's dad on the way back.

When we got home, all of us went inside our houses to change clothes. Dad asked Mom if we could take her minivan to get lunch since we could now get it out of the garage. Brian, Dan, and my family piled in and went to a good hamburger place and stuffed our faces. I thought about throwing a French fry at Sean, but I was too busy eating. The men talked about maybe going to a Rockies game together soon.

Even though Brian had changed his shirt, I still could see a big red 'C' on his chest. I still felt uneasy about it. But what could I do? I didn't know why this was happening. I thought if I told Brian's dad, he would just think I was weird.

When we got back home, Brian and his dad went on to their house. Dad and Sean and I went inside. The house smelled wonderful. Mom had baked a cherry pie while we worked outdoors.

"Phew. You guys stink," Mom said when Dad hugged her.

"That was a lot of hard work," Dad said.

"Thank you for doing it. It was nice of Dan and Brian to help. Now I can get my car out of the garage. All of you take a shower and put on clean clothes. Except for you, Ozzie. Then we can have dessert," she said with a laugh, patting Ozzie's head.

Cherry pie is my favorite. We had vanilla ice cream too.

Dessert was almost enough to make me forget about the red C, but I couldn't stop picturing it on Brian's shirt every time I thought about the busy day we'd had.

CHAPTER SIX

SEAN and I go to a small Montessori school. Grades four through six are combined in one classroom. That allows me and Sean to be together most of the school day. I like interacting with the upper grades, and I can help with Sean when he starts fidgeting during his classes. The teachers know what to do, but I think it helps him for me to be near. I can look at him across the room and send him love through my eyes. Ozzie is with him at all times, too.

The classroom has small tables arranged in a circle because that makes talking easy. The walls are lined with shelves full of books for readers our ages. We can choose books from these shelves to read during quiet time. There are also whiteboards all around. The wooden floor is mostly covered with a bright blue and orange and grey rug. We used to go to another school where desks were arranged in rows. I like the circle design better. It makes me feel like we are all in this together, somehow, instead of separated. I can look at the face of each person as they respond to the teacher.

On one warm, sunny day, right after the whole school partici- pated in reciting the Pledge of Allegiance to the flag, like we do every day, Sean and the other sixth graders left the classroom to get their school pictures taken. The fifth graders went to music class. While they were gone, my teacher, Mrs. Stein, called my class, the fourth graders, into another circle where we studied writing composition. I love this subject the most. I love to write, and I already work on the school newspaper. Today we worked on learning how to write a topic sentence. This was easy for me.

While it wasn't my turn to read my topic sentence, my thoughts wandered. I felt myself pop out of my body. I flashed on an imaginary scene on the front steps of the school where I saw in my mind a fifth grader get pushed by a sixth grader. He slipped on the concrete and fell, skinning his knees. After all of us fourth graders finished the writing composition exercise, we moved on to math with the assistant teacher, Miss Millhone. Before I started on my math worksheet, I told our main teacher, Mrs. Stein, about my vision.

"I saw Randall slip on the steps and fall after Steven bumped him. Steven was calling Randall a know-it-all because he always knows the answers in class. Randall hurt his knees," I said.

"Noah, nothing like that has happened. We teach all the students to treat each other with compassion. We are all different, each in our own way."

I knew Mrs. Stein would not believe me. But I felt I had to tell her, just the same. I knew my vision was going to happen, and I'd hoped she'd be able to stop Randall from getting hurt. I looked down so she wouldn't see the disappointment on my face. It seems like I am so different from everyone else. I wish things were really like Mrs. Stein said, that each of us could just be who we are, different, but the same, and that this would be okay with everyone.

Then, during recess, when the nearby teacher was distracted, it happened just the way I saw it. Steven brushed against Randall, causing him to fall down the steps. Randall's jeans were torn on the knees. He yelped, then wiped at his eyes. I guess he didn't want anyone to see his tears. I'm sure his knees must have been bloody, but he acted like nothing happened. None of the adults saw it, and Randall didn't tell. I didn't tell, either. I didn't want to be the next one to be bullied by Steven. I looked away and pretended I saw nothing. Randall looked up at me though, and I felt guilty for not helping him. Silently, just moving my mouth, I said "sorry" to him. He had an angry look on his face and his eyes locked with mine with an accusing look. He didn't dare look at Steven. Other kids make fun of me because I talk about weird ideas and because I'm short. I don't know what to do about that. Telling gets me nowhere, though.

I went down the steps behind Randall and out to the playground. The school always provides a big snack bowl on a table for us at recess. After munching a bunch of grapes from the bowl, I found a baseball in the sports equipment room and asked Brian if he wanted to play pitch. While we tossed the ball, I missed some of Brian's pitches and wobbled others. Brian never missed a ball. Never wobbled. He is brilliant in every way, I think. Sure of himself. I admire him. I wish I was sure of myself like he is. He is like a hero to me. But still, the big red 'C' on his chest. *Why?*

Brian is the pitcher on the Little League baseball team on which I am the catcher, so we need to practice together as much as possible, both during school and after classes. Then we practice with the whole team three days a week. We two are the only players on the team who attend the Montessori school. The rest of the team attends a nearby public elementary school. Sometimes, we have actual games after school, but most of the time, either we travel to another school on a bus, or they come to our school. Those games have to be on Saturdays.

CHAPTER SEVEN

THE NEXT SATURDAY, my team, the Bulldogs, had a game. We played the Eagles, a team from across town. The sun was burning down on the red-orange crushed pebble baseball diamond. The grass all around the infield was bright green. I was made catcher because I am short and fast. I am also the leadoff batter for the same reasons. Since I am so short, I have a narrow strike zone and pitchers usually walk me. Because I am fast, I can get away with stealing bases. In fact, I've never been thrown out. I think this is kind of cool, but I wish I could have more chances to hit the ball. I asked Coach Owens about this one day.

"Coach, I would like more chances to hit the ball," I said.

"I would like that, too, but the fact is, pitchers can't hit your strike zone very often. This is an advantage to the team because you get on base a lot. I love to see you on base because I know you are fast and you can steal bases easily," he explained.

"That sort of seems like cheating," I said.

"No, it is called strategy. All coaches have a plan for winning," he said.

As the catcher, I have a view of the complete field. I am aware of what all other players are doing. I can warn the pitcher if someone is about to steal a base. I think being catcher is fun, except that it is hot. And all that gear is a lot of trouble to get into—knee pads, chest protector, and face mask. It's clumsy.

Even though it was spring that day and the temperature stayed in the 70s, the heat of the sun burned my skin through my red Bulldogs T-shirt. I could feel it through the thin air, not much oxygen, at our altitude of one mile above sea level. Sweat poured down my face. I could taste the salt in it.

I could also smell myself—stinky. I never used to notice when I got stinky, but one day, I heard a girl at school telling another girl that she wished I would wear deodorant. I felt embarrassed. Mom said she would get me some. She said that stinky underarms meant I was growing up. She forgot to get it when she went to the store, though.

Pow! A batter on the Eagles team hit the ball straight up in the air. I saw it headed backwards toward me, but over my head. As I pulled off my clunky mask with one hand so I could see it, I adjusted my position and held my gloved hand above my head because I saw the ball arced backwards and to the left. I jumped that way and grabbed it. All that took about three seconds. It felt like a long time, like I was moving in slow motion.

I caught his foul ball before it hit the ground, and the batter was out. All my teammates yelled congratulations. So did Mom from the stands. She comes to every game. Sean and Ozzie come, too, and Sean was yelling along with Mom. Dad is usually at work.

At my next at bat, I got walked, as usual. While the Eagles pitcher tried to throw our next batter, Brian, out, I stole second base. I slid right under the second baseman, red dust flying everywhere. There was so much dust, he couldn't even see me for a moment. He didn't tag me in time.

Then Brian smacked the ball right toward second base, but I took off for third. Brian made it to first and while the Eagle players were trying to tag him, I dashed to third base. Brian kept going so he was now on second.

"Yay! Way to go, Brian," I shouted to my friend.

Everybody on our team and in the stands was stomping, dancing around, and yelling with glee. There I was, on third, with Brian on second. I was tense, holding my breath as the next batter, Joey, took two strikes and passed on two balls. The next pitch would be it. Then Joey smacked the ball down first base line. He was tagged out, but I made it home. That was the first out of the inning. I was so excited to make the first score of the game for the Bulldogs. The team and crowd cheered like crazy.

Brian was now on third. I knew the next batter, Bobby, a sixth grader, could hit the ball hard. He hit a pop fly and the Eagles pitcher caught it, so that was out number two. Brian did not advance.

The next batter, Hunter, struck out. Darn. He usually got a hit. That was out number three. Brian was left on base.

After a couple of long innings under the scorching sun, nothing else happened. Some batters got walked. My mind wandered from the action. I saw in my mind that a batter on the Eagles team was going to hit a ball hard and that it would hit one of my team members in the head, knocking him out. I signaled to Coach Owens for a time-out and told him what I saw.

"Soon an Eagles batter is going to hit a ball that will knock out Tommy at first base," I said.

"He'd have to really hit it hard, Noah. I don't think that will happen," said Mr. Owens.

I felt alone and bent down, scraping the dirt off home plate with my fingers. The umpire has a brush for that, but I just didn't want anyone to see my face. No one *ever* believes me. I kept looking down so no one would see how discouraged I felt.

The next time the Eagles came to bat, the first kid up smacked one of Brian's balls right down the first base line and into the side of Tommy's head. He fell head-first into the red dust of the infield. For a moment everything went silent as I realized another vision had come true. But as I thought about the cry Tommy gave, before he fell to the ground, I felt terrible that my vision had been correct. Everyone, including me, rushed to help. I had to throw off my gear first. His mom ran sobbing onto the field. Someone must have called an ambulance because soon sirens could be heard, getting louder and louder as the truck bounced down a dirt hill to get to the field. The driver stayed in the ambulance, ready to roll, while two paramedics dashed to the form of Tommy, still lying in the dirt. One was carrying a backboard. As they gave first aid to Tommy, I heard his mom, Iris, call his dad on her cell phone. The paramedics got Tommy onto the board and put braces around his head to keep him still. Tommy's mom got into the ambulance with her boy. He was taken to the emergency room at the hospital.

I felt miserable because Tommy was hurt, but also because the coach did not believe me when I told him this would happen. I don't think he even remembered I had told him Tommy would get hit by a ball. He was too busy calming the team and getting us re-organized.

The game had passed the five-inning mark, so the umpire called an end to it because everyone was upset about Tommy getting hit. The Eagles won by one run. This was the first loss of the season for the Bulldogs. On top of Tommy getting hurt, we also had to lose the game. I was dragging my arms, my glove almost touching the ground, as I walked over to Mom, Sean, and Ozzie in the stands. She hugged me and asked if I would like to go for ice cream.

"I don't feel like ice cream," I said, still feeling dejected.

She looked into my eyes, knowing the day I turned down ice cream, there must be something very wrong.

"Tell me how you are feeling," she said.

"Well, I had a vision that Tommy was going to be hit in the head with a ball. I told the coach about it, but he just ignored me. I wish people would believe me when I get visions and dreams."

Mom looked at me in a peculiar way, like she was trying to figure out how to help me but had no clue.

"It would be nice and cold and yummy. We could get out of this heat for a few minutes," she coaxed.

"Well, okay," I said, feeling brighter at the thought.

We went to the Dairy Queen. While Mom ordered chocolate sundaes for us, I went in the bathroom and splashed cold water on my face and head. That felt good, too. I came out dripping, my hair sticking up all over. Mom cracked up laughing at the sight of me. I think she looks pretty when she laughs. I scooped up some ice cream on a spoon and got some of it on my nose. Sean gave some of his ice cream to Ozzie. Since he is a therapy dog, he gets to go into restaurants. She laughed even harder. When we finished our sundaes, I licked my spoon clean and stuck it on my nose, making a silly face. She thought that was funny, too, which was what I intended. The stress of the game and Tommy's injury seemed to slide away.

Once we got home, Dad was there. Mom called Tommy's mom, Iris, on her cell phone to ask if Tommy was okay. She put the phone on speaker so I could hear, too.

"He'll be fine. He has a mild concussion, but his skull isn't cracked. We just have to watch him overnight," said Tommy's mom.

"Let me know if I can help in any way," said Mom.

As Mom hung up the phone, she patted me on the shoulder. "Tommy is going to be fine. Everything will be okay." I wanted to believe her, that everything would be okay, but I couldn't stop thinking about the visions and dreams I constantly had. No one would believe me. I could have stopped Tommy from being injured. We could have had a chance at winning the game if he hadn't been hurt. I wish grownups would listen to me. I feel like no one listens because I'm a kid. If I were a grownup, would people believe me?

CHAPTER EIGHT

A COUPLE OF DAYS LATER, after school, I went out in the sunshine for a while to ride my blue *Speed Racer* bike on the sidewalk. I saw a couple of my friends skateboarding. Randy and Johnny live four doors down from our house. They were headed for the park, which is bordered all around with old oak trees. At one end of the park is a playground with sliding boards, a sandbox, swings and a merry-go-round to play on. At the other end, there is a wired fence that encloses what used to be a tennis court. Now, there are a couple of half-pipes built for skateboarders.

"Hey Noah," Johnny said, "do you want to go over to the half-pipes with us?"

"Nah. On Friday, I was skateboarding home from baseball practice and I hit a tree root that was just up through a crack in the sidewalk. I broke a wheel on my board," I said.

"Did you get hurt?" Randy asked.

"Nah. Just a few scratches. I was wearing pads. But now I have to replace the wheel," I said.

We talked a while about Rockies baseball.

"The season is about to start. I can't wait to go to a game," I said.

"Yeah. I think they have good players this year," Randy said.

"Carlos Gonzales was a free agent, but before he could get away, they signed him on again," I said.

"I'm sure glad. The team wouldn't be nearly as good without CarGo," Johnny said.

"Maybe we can get our parents to take all of us to a game," Randy said.

"That would be a blast. Maybe I could catch a ball," I said.

Soon, those two brothers went on to the park.

When I came in after about an hour, I was hot and sweaty again. Not as bad as when we were loading wood, but still icky. I walked through the mudroom, past the candy apple red washer and dryer. I saw that my parents were sitting together in the nook, talking. They were using quiet tones, but as I walked past on my way to my room, I heard the word 'money.'

I went to my room and took off my sweaty tennis shoes and socks and swished my damp shirt against my body. The air-conditioning was on so I knew I would dry out soon. I sat back on my bed and started playing Police Procedures. After an hour, I noticed I was fidgeting while I thought of next moves. Maybe hearing Mom and Dad talk about money in worried tones was bothering me.

My mind began to drift from the game and then I guess I fell asleep because suddenly I could see that I was out of my body. It was a strange experience to watch myself walking home from the library one day, wearing my short sleeve *Transformers* T-shirt and long jeans and carrying a backpack. In my dream, I saw a man I thought I recognized from one of the posters at the police station.

The man had shoulder-length dirty blond hair and had a scruffy beard and mustache. He wore a filthy plaid shirt and jeans shiny with grease. His black tennis shoes looked ratty. I saw myself hide behind greenish-looking lilac bushes, just leafing out. I pulled out my phone to call 911. Officer Chavez answered.

"Officer Chavez, this is Noah Muller. I just saw a man who

looks like one on your wanted posters; one that is wanted for armed robbery," I said. I was trying to speak in a soft voice, but I was so excited.

"Where are you, Noah?" she asked in a panicked voice.

"I'm on Tayler Street, two blocks south of the library. I'm hiding behind some lilac bushes," I whispered in my vision.

"Stay hidden. Don't approach the man. An officer will be right there," said the sergeant.

"Don't worry. I'm not moving," I said.

My usual impulse was to disobey an order if I thought I knew best. I moved. I jumped from behind the bushes and took a picture of the man, then texted it to Officer Chavez.

In my vision, the man saw me doing this and began to run after me. I ran as fast as I could, right past an arriving patrol car. I stuck my phone in my pocket. The big man grabbed me and turned in a different direction, dragging me. I dreamed I was kicking and screaming, trying to get away. My backpack fell to the sidewalk. Books and paper splayed out. The officers gave chase, racing through the neighborhood past houses with green lawns and flower beds in bloom.

People walking on the sidewalk jumped out of our way. I saw one young woman in jeans, a T-shirt and tennis shoes pushing a pink baby carriage. She fell to the ground, her arms around the stroller, her head down. The baby screamed. I bit the man hard on his hand and he yelped, flinging me aside. I fell with a thump onto the sidewalk. I landed on my hands and knees and rolled. Right then, I saw an officer jump on the bad guy. Both hit the ground. The officer put his knee in the criminal's back to keep him still and handcuffed him. He jerked the man to his feet and shoved him in a patrol car. Then he looked to see if I was hurt.

"Are you okay, Noah?" he asked, putting his hand on my shoulder.

In my dream, I was shaking all over, but I was not wounded badly. I had a few scratches on my hands from hitting the pavement, and that hurt. My jeans protected my knees, but they got ripped.

Another patrolman took me to the station where I was again examined by Officer Chavez. I was congratulated for my help. She applied first aid stuff to my scratches.

"C'mon over here, Noah. I want a picture of me standing with a real hero," Officer Chavez said. I thought she'd be mad at me for not doing what she told me when she said for me to stay put, but she didn't seem to be. I wondered if she was trying to make me feel better since she had not believed this could happen. I walked over, grinning. I had almost quit shaking, but I still felt kinda scared. I saw a television reporter in the station, asking about another situation. Sounded like she was talking to the sergeant about some report of a shooting in town. She asked Officer Chavez my name, then introduced herself.

"Hi. I'm Brenda Sloan," the blonde woman said to me. "Mind if my camera guy takes your picture while we talk?"

I was overwhelmed and said nothing.

"Tell me what happened, Noah."

"I was walking home from the library and I saw a man that looked like one I've seen before on a wanted poster," I said.

"Where did you see the poster?"

"Here in the station, on the wall. I come here sometimes and talk to the officers if they are not busy. I want to be a policeman."

"Tell me what happened when you saw the man."

"I called Officer Chavez and told her. I took his picture with my phone. Then he saw me and grabbed me and ran."

"I would have been terrified. How did you feel?"

"That was it. Terrified."

"Congratulations on a job well done," she said as the cameraman filmed.

Other officers shook my hand and patted my back. Mom was called to pick me up. She left Sean and Ozzie at home and came quick. She was shocked.

"Noah, I can't believe you did such a thing. We will talk about how dangerous that was when we get home. I'm proud of you, though. You helped the police," she said in a worried tone.

She wrapped her arms around me. That's when I lost it. I started crying.

Mom kept hugging me and stroking my back and hair.

"You're safe now. You're okay. Let's get you home."

Officer Chavez handed Mom a box of tissues. She grabbed a couple and started wiping my face.

"Here, Noah, blow your nose," she said as she continued to stroke my back. Another officer held a little trash can for the used tissues. I began to calm down.

I saw the reporter talking to Mom to make sure it was okay to have interviewed and filmed me.

Once home, Mom called Dad.

"You won't believe what Noah did today," she said, her voice still full of worry.

"What happened?" asked Dad. Mom was so excited, she talked loud and I could hear Dad's concerned response, also loud.

"He helped the police capture a wanted man," she said. She related the events of the day.

Dad asked to talk to me.

"Noah, you could have been killed," he lectured.

"I know. But you would have done the same," I replied.

He then congratulated me on my quick thinking and action.

"What would you like to do to celebrate how brave you are?"

I didn't think I needed to be rewarded for doing something anyone would do in that situation, but I was not going to pass a chance to do something fun. I heard Sean call my name and popped back into my body. Whew, what an adventure. It was the most detailed dream I ever remember having. But I didn't think it would happen in real life. I didn't talk about it to anyone.

CHAPTER NINE

I LOOKED up to see Sean and Ozzie walking past my door. I don't know where they had been. Maybe Sean took Ozzie for a walk. He has to do that two times a day, even though we have a fenced backyard for the dog. Ozzie doesn't like to be outside by himself much. His job is to stand by Sean at all times.

Feeling restless after that vision, I followed them to Sean's room and watched while he worked on a new project. Sean was sitting on the floor in front of the table he calls his lab. Ozzie was lying by his feet. He had a small wrench in his hand. Mom and Dad had given him a set of tiny silver tools called Allen wrenches because he likes to work on small things. He also had a little can of some kind of oil and a white cleaning cloth that was soft so it wouldn't scratch glass surfaces.

"Are you working on Mom's old computer?" I asked.

I was aware that Mom's old black Toshiba computer had quit working and she had bought a new one last week.

"Yeah. I bet if I take it all apart, I can figure out what is wrong," he said.

I watched, still twitching with excess energy. You'd think I'd be worn out from school and bike riding, but instead, I was hyped. Sean inspected each piece of the computer as he took it apart, wiggling things that had movable hinges or joints.

"Look—this switch is stuck!" he exclaimed.

He cleaned it and then it moved freely. He put the computer back together.

"How do you remember where each part goes?" I asked.

"It's just how my mind sees things," he replied.

I wish people would understand how my mind works the way they understand Sean. He has a knack for mechanical stuff. He turned the computer on and it worked.

"Mom, look. Your old computer is fixed," he yelled with excitement.

She and Dad came into the room.

"That's great, Sean. You are so smart," she said.

Ozzie wagged his tail from where he sat next to Sean.

"I'm happy for Sean, too," Ozzie said to me in my mind.

I smiled at Ozzie, showing him I understood what he said. I could read his body language, too.

I saw how Mom was impressed. She sort of reached her arms out toward Sean. I knew she wished she could give him a hug. But both she and I knew he wouldn't like that. He didn't like to be touched.

"That's amazing work, Sean," Dad said.

"This is what was wrong," Sean said, as he pointed out the switch that had been stuck. "It was just dirty," he said.

"Would you like to have this old computer?" Mom asked. Her voice sounded proud of him. I think she wanted to make up for the lack of a hug.

"Wow, that would be fun. I could download software that would let me design things," he said, twisting his body a bit like he does when he gets excited.

As I looked on, I admired Sean's genius, but I also felt left out because Sean always got all the attention. No one wanted to hear from me. They got uncomfortable when I talked about stuff I saw in my mind or in dreams. With the spotlight always on

Sean, I felt even more alone. I looked away so they didn't see that I felt bad. I was also jealous that Sean got a computer and I didn't. I went back to my own room and started playing Police Procedures again.

Later, after getting past my bad feelings, I went back to Sean's room. He was focused on his robot project.

"How are you doing with your design?" I asked.

"I think the design is complete. Look, I can put gears here, here, and here that will enable the robot to move." Dad had given him some round brass clasps from his stash of office supplies he keeps at home. Those would allow things to move in circles.

Sean pretty much only has construction paper and glue to build with, but I know he hopes someday to get materials to make a robot that works. I hope he does, too. That would be so cool.

I wanted to ask Sean if he had noticed Mom looking far away and sad sometimes, but he was focused on his project. Maybe I would talk to him about this later. I went to my own room, alone. I got my science book and went to the nook to do more homework. We were studying weather, which fascinated me. I liked learning how storms develop, especially since we just had a big one.

CHAPTER TEN

BECAUSE OF HIS DISORDER, Sean usually kept to himself on the playground, along with Ozzie. I'm a friendly kind of guy, but I'm bullied because I'm small and because I talk about weird things I see in my mind. I wish people understood me. I wish people would believe me. I only tell people about the visions so they can stop bad things happening. But no one ever listens. On this warm day, my friend Leah and I were talking during recess.

"Were you scared when the lights went out during the storm last week?" Leah asked.

"Yeah, I was at first. Lightning struck a tree in our yard and it split open. Most of it fell across our driveway with a horrible crash," I said.

"Wow. I was scared, too, but nothing got hit in our yard," she said.

"The thing is, I saw that the tree was going to get hit before it happened. I told my mom, but she didn't believe me."

As I was telling Leah about the vision, two bigger boys walked past. They looked at me with smirking eyes and mean faces.

I knew bullying would not happen on the school grounds, but when I walked home after baseball practice, I was open to attack. Usually Sean and Ozzie hang out with me at practice, then we walk home together. But on this day, Sean had a meeting of his Mathletics Club after school.

I was wearing my favorite Jimmy Johnson T-shirt, jeans and black tennis shoes that lit up with each step as I walked off the baseball field at the end of practice. I noticed the sweet scent of the pink roses in somebody's yard along the sidewalk. I also noticed the two big boys who heard me talking to Leah, Steven and his friend Cecil. They walked up to me and started shoving me around and calling me names.

"You're a weirdo," Steven, wearing black tennis shoes, jeans, and a Twenty One Pilots band T-shirt, shouted as he pushed me across a nearby flower garden. I stumbled backward and against a wooden fence.

"Leave me alone," I yelled, struggling to stay on my feet. Fear sweat was popping out on my forehead.

"And you look like a little baby," shouted Cecil, wearing black tennis shoes, jeans, and a *Transformers* T-shirt. He also pushed me, and I fell on my butt, my back against the fence.

Out of the corner of my eye, I noticed Leah, who'd been watching practice. She was wearing a blue dress, her long brown hair hanging loose over her shoulders. I saw she was videoing the whole event with her phone. She stayed back out of the fight and kept filming.

Sean, coming from his Mathletics Club meeting, saw this and jumped to my defense. I could see he was going to whop the bigger bully, but Ozzie dashed in front of him, barking. The bullies ran from the dog. I got up and wiped dirt and sweat off my face with the edge of my T-shirt.

"Are you okay?" Sean asked.

"Yeah. Just scared," I said.

Leah messaged the video to me, proof the bullies started the fight.

I heard the video pop up on my phone, which was in my back

pocket. I pulled out my phone and she, Sean, Ozzie, and I watched it right quick.

"Thank you, Leah," I said, my voice filled with relief and gratitude.

"You're welcome. I'm glad I was here. Tomorrow, we will show it to the principal, Mr. Andrews. Those boys will be in trouble," she said.

"Thanks for sticking up for me," I said to Sean.

"You're a pest but you *are* my brother," replied Sean.

"Well, thanks."

"You're welcome. Really, it was Ozzie who scared them off."

Me and Sean look out for each other.

A small breeze began to blow from the West as we walked Leah to her house. That cooled us off a bit. Ozzie strutted along beside Sean, but he kept glancing over at me. I thought he was double-checking that I was okay. We came to Leah's house. I noticed it was painted light blue and had dark blue trim. I saw that flowers of all colors and types bloomed along the sidewalk as we walked toward her wide front porch. A swing, hanging from the porch overhead, swayed in a gentle breeze.

"Would you like to come inside? I bet my mom has fresh lemonade in the fridge," asked Leah.

"Thanks, but we better get home. It is getting late," Sean responded.

"Aw, Sean. Lemonade would be good," I said to him.

"Noah, you are a mess. We need to get you home," he said. He sounded like my mom when he said that.

We walked on home. When we got there, Mom looked at me with dismay.

"Noah, what happened to you? You are a mess," said Mom, not knowing she was repeating Sean's description of me.

"Some bigger boys jumped on me after baseball practice. They called me names and pushed me into a fence. Sean and Ozzie were coming from Mathletics and they saw what was happening. Sean was ready to beat the crap out of the bullies, but Ozzie snarled at them. They ran away," I said. As I related the story, my voice started trembling. My terror came back to me and I popped some tears. Mom put her arms around me. Sean got a wet cloth from the bathroom so I could wash my face. Ozzie whimpered. It seemed I was making him sad, too.

"I'm glad that Sean was there to help. But why were those boys calling you names and pushing you around?" she asked

"The kids pick on me because sometimes I talk about dreams and stuff I see in my mind."

"Keep those things to yourself. You think these things happen to everyone but really, no one knows what you are talking about," she said. Even my mom thought I was weird.

"Leah videoed the whole thing," I said as I showed her my phone.

After she watched, she said, "Well, we'll talk to the principal tomorrow. Those boys are in for it."

I felt depressed and alone. Even my own mother didn't understand. But I went to take a shower, so she didn't see my disappointment.

The next day, Mom, Leah, and I showed the video to Mr. Andrews and Mrs. Stein.

"You can see clearly that the boys attacked Noah for no reason," Mom said.

"You are right. Noah, I'm sorry this happened to you. I will talk to their parents and they will be punished," Mr. Andrews said.

The next day, after all the students in the school said the Pledge of Allegiance first thing, we all got a big lecture.

"All of you know we don't tolerate bullying here," Mr. Andrews said. "All of us are different. Each of us has our own history, our own beliefs, our own ways of relating to life." I listened as Mr. Andrews talked about how we are all different. It made me happy to think he understands how I have a different way of relating to life. If I told him about my visions, would he believe me? I almost started to think he would, but I'd told so many people before him and the ones who should believe me don't. My own parents don't even believe me. I decided I should finish listening to Mr. Andrews talk.

"Those boys will be suspended for three days. Their grades will be affected. It is important to always treat each other with respect. Go to your classes now."

CHAPTER ELEVEN

THE WEEKEND WAS COMING UP. The weather girl on TV said the weather would be extra warm for late April. Sean and I wanted to go to the IMAX Theater to see the movie *Ready Player One*. I heard it was a scary movie, but I wasn't going to tell Mom that. I like being terrified.

After school, we approached Mom while she was cooking dinner. "Can we go to the IMAX and see *Ready Player One?*" I asked.

"Yeah, Mom, I can't wait to see that movie," Sean added.

"This is the latest science fiction show?" asked Mom, stirring something that smelled good in a big pot. "What is it about, anyway?" I knew she was clueless.

"It takes place in 2045. There are game players who are competing to get control over a virtual reality world game called Oasis that is worth billions of dollars. The Oasis is like a perfect Earth, all green and clean and safe. The good guys want to prevent control of the Oasis from getting into the hands of an evil corporation. Whoever wins is in charge of the virtual world. It's supposed to be good," Sean explained.

While he was explaining the plot, I felt myself pop out of my body. I felt like I was floating above myself. In my mind, I saw myself being captured by an evil looking robot. While I was still in the midst of trying to get away, I popped back into my body. I heard Mom and Sean still talking, so I must not have been out long. It seemed like an hour while I tried to get away, but it must have been seconds. I wish I understood how this happened, and if I traveled through time.

"And this is for kids?" Mom asked.

"Yeah. The main warrior is a teenage boy," Sean replied.

"Well, okay. If Dad wants to go, we'll do it Friday night. Between now and then, I'll get some earplugs," she said, smiling.

"Thanks, Mom," both of us shouted at the same time.

When Dad came home, he and Mom discussed the movie.

"I need to work late so I don't have to go in on Saturday. You go ahead and take the boys and Ozzie," he said to Mom.

"Well, okay," she replied. She sounded disappointed.

Sean and I asked if we could go to the IMAX inside the Denver Museum.

"Why that one?" she asked.

"The screen is three stories high. I think it is the biggest in the city," Sean said.

"Mom, can we get tickets to go to the museum after the movie?" I asked.

"Not at night. The museum is only open until five. We can have a snack before we go. Then after the movie, maybe Dad could meet us some place nice for dinner," she said.

"That'd be good. Can we go to Chili's?" Sean said. His fave.

"We'll see how it goes," Mom said.

The drive to the museum in the middle of town takes a while since we live in a suburb. As Mom dealt with traffic, I felt myself pop out of my body. It was like I was floating above myself, looking down at me doing something else. I saw me inside a scene where I was fighting off robots trying to take over the world. Suddenly, I popped back into my body as Mom hit the brakes hard to keep from hitting a young dog that was crossing the busy road. The tires screeched. Ozzie bumped his chin on the back of Mom's seat as he reached out a paw to catch himself.

"Mom, we almost hit that puppy. Ozzie hit his head," Sean said.

"I know, but we didn't. And Ozzie is okay, too," she replied as she glanced back at the dog.

"Do you think it belongs to somebody?" I asked.

"Yes. I see a collar and a tag. He doesn't look hungry," she said.

"I wish people would take better care of their animals. He shouldn't be running loose," I said.

It got to be time to go inside the IMAX. Sean and I were on good behavior. Ozzie is always on good behavior. He got to go with us because he is a therapy dog. We walked in from the hot evening into the cool, darkened theater. The cold air felt nice. All around, the inside was made of dull copper and white marble. There were fancy lamps hanging from the ceiling. Right away, I smelled popcorn.

"Can we have popcorn?" I asked.

"Sure," Mom replied.

She bought a buttery bag for each of us. Well, not one for Ozzie. We climbed the stairs to the seating area. My eyes popped when I saw that gigantic screen.

We got seats on the third row. The movie was just beginning by the time we sat down. Soon, screaming and crashing noises filled the surround sound theater. Sean and I sat with our mouths hanging open. But soon I saw Ozzie give Mom a pleading look.

"Mom, I think the screeching noise is hurting Ozzie's ears," I told her.

Mom looked at Ozzie. "You're right. I'm going to sit in the lobby with Ozzie," she told us.

I bet her ears were hurting, too. Maybe even her head. I was glad she wasn't going to see the horror parts, though. She might have gotten mad that I didn't exactly tell her the truth about it.

As soon as Mom was out of sight, I thought of throwing popcorn at Sean, but I forgot that idea. Soon, it seemed I had popped out of my body again. I felt like I was captured by an evil warrior. I was screaming for help. Before any help came, I popped back into my body. I think I must have had that experience because of the terror I felt as I watched the movie. But that did not help me understand why this kind of thing happens during other kinds of experiences.

Both Sean and I babbled about the movie all the way home.

"I'm sure glad the good guys won," I said.

"Yeah. It seemed like the movie was saying that if the good warriors won, they not only got control of the Oasis but would also be able to make our real world a better place," Sean said.

He's brainy like that.

Dad met us at Chili's. I ordered my favorite, Baby Back Ribs. Sean and Mom both like Margarita Chicken. Dad had a steak. The restaurant was noisy, but I forgot to notice that when our food came. Everything looked and smelled delicious.

"How did you like the movie?" Dad asked.

I didn't want to tell him about my experience out of my body. He would not have believed me, anyway.

"Ozzie and I had to sit in the lobby. The noise hurt both our ears," Mom said. Dad chuckled, like he knew what she meant.

"I loved the movie. The good guys won the Oasis and planned to use it as a model for helping Earth improve," I said.

"I'm not going to tell you the ending. You and Mom might want to see it later," Sean said. I saw Mom and Dad roll their eyes at each other.

He wasn't the only one not telling them what happened. I wasn't going to talk about things that I didn't understand myself. I don't know what the experience about being captured by an evil warrior has to do with anything happening in real life. I wanted to know more but I didn't know who to ask. I felt frustrated and confused.

I wished I could go to the library and find a book about evil warriors, but none of them would be real. Why would I have a vision of being captured if it couldn't happen? With every vision I had coming true, this had to be telling me something evil was going to happen. I would need to keep my eyes open, and maybe stay close to Sean and Ozzie for protection.

CHAPTER TWELVE

MONDAY WAS SCORCHING HOT AGAIN. We had a short day at school and were home by noon. Mom fixed deli ham sandwiches and potato chips for lunch.

While I munched my sandwich, I asked, "Can we go to the pool today, Mom?"

"Well, not just yet. The sun's too hot and you'd burn no matter what we put on you. How about in a couple of hours?"

"Okay. Guess I'll just play video games," I said.

"I'm going to the grocery store. Can you two *behave?*"

"Sure, Mom. We always behave," I said.

I saw her roll her eyes.

We sat in front of the big screen television and played the car chase game for a while. I got bored and punched Sean in the arm, causing him to miss a turn in the video with his virtual Corvette and skid off-road, ending the game.

"Look what you made me do, you brat!" shouted Sean, frustrated.

Then he piled onto me, pummeling me with his fists. Sean is slow to get mad, but then he snaps.

"Ow," I yelled, hitting back.

We were wrestling on the floor when I heard Mom slam the

car door. I backed away from Sean and we both were quietly playing a new game by the time she walked into the kitchen with arms full of grocery bags. Mom looked in on us.

"What have you guys been doing?" she asked me, a look of suspicion on her face.

"Oh, just playing *Car Chase*," I said, an innocent look on my face.

She stared at me hard to see if she could believe me.

"Can we go to the pool now?" Sean asked.

"I guess it is cool enough to not burn you to a crisp," she replied.

We put on our swim trunks and rode our bikes to the nearby pool. Ozzie ran beside us. The pool was part of a recreation complex. There was a soccer field where the high school teams played, a tennis court, also for the big kids, a pool for adults and older kids like me with a short diving board and a tall one, and a baby pool. Though he loved water, Ozzie was not allowed in the pool. He sat under a shady tree and watched us.

As I floated in the water in the adult pool, I felt myself pop out of my body again. In my mind, I saw a toddler in the baby pool floundering in the water, like he couldn't quite stay on his feet. I popped back in and looked at the little pool. Sure enough, there was a little boy about two years old splashing around like he couldn't stay up. His head kept going under the water. His big sister was supposed to be watching him, I think, but she was yakking with girlfriends while he was gasping. I climbed out and ran to him, jerking him up under his little arms. As I pulled him out, he was crying.

"Hey, are you his sister?" I yelled at the girl.

"Oh no, what happened?" she asked as she dashed to the little boy and put her arms around him.

By this time, the lifeguard had dashed over to us.

"He was not able to stay on his feet in the water. He almost drowned," I replied.

"You saved him," the lifeguard, Johnny, said, appreciation in his voice.

"Yeah. Well, his sister wasn't looking," I said. After I said the words, I felt bad for making his sister sound bad. I thought about telling the lifeguard I had a vision of the boy drowning, but I decided not to because it would just be one more person looking at me as though I were strange.

I turned and went back to the water to play with Sean. We were so happy to be in the cool water. We had forgotten about the fight earlier in the day. As time passed, however, I couldn't resist splashing water into Sean's face. The fight was on again.

The lifeguard spotted Sean trying to hold my face under water and jumped in to get us.

"Stop! Both of you. Out of the pool now!" he commanded as he pulled us apart. He called Mom to pick us up.

When Mom arrived, the lifeguard ratted us out.

"The boys were fighting in the water. I saw the big one holding the head of the little one under the water," he said to her. Only moments before I was a hero for having saved a boy's life. Now the lifeguard was looking at me as though I were a problem child. It was a good thing I didn't tell him about popping out of my body. He'd probably rat me out for that as well.

"Sean, why would you do such a thing?" she demanded.

"Noah is always starting fights, Mom," said Sean.

"That's no excuse. You tried to kill him!" she yelled.

"No, Mom. I would have let him up before he was in real trouble," Sean said.

"You don't know that. You are bigger than him. You don't know how much stronger you are. No video games for a week," she ranted.

Sean looked down while she was yelling but as soon as she turned her back, he gave me the evil eye. I figured this fight wasn't over.

We loaded our bikes into the trunk of her minivan.

I knew Mom was furious. And I knew I had caused the problem. I just couldn't resist acting out my jealousy of Sean, though.
I was always jealous of him getting all the attention, even now
when the attention wasn't a good thing. I carried that feeling
with me all the time, even if he wasn't the center of attention at
the moment. I wondered again if my being a brat could be the
reason why Mom sometimes does not look happy.

"Noah saved the life of a little boy," Sean said.

Mom turned to glance at me before she had to look back at
the road. "Did you save a little boy, Noah?"

I wanted to tell her about having a vision that the boy was in
trouble and that was why I was able to help, but I didn't want
talk about it anymore. I knew she wouldn't believe me, anyway. I
kept my face down so no one would see my feelings. Besides, I
thought Sean was just trying to butter her up. I mumbled a
response. "No big deal." If I couldn't tell the whole story, I didn't
want to tell any of it.

I didn't feel like a hero as Mom's anger festered. "Both of you
change clothes and stay in your rooms," she ordered.

I heard her calling Dad. I'm sure she ratted us out to him.
Soon, he was home.

"Sean, Noah—get in here," he commanded.

We walked from our rooms into the living room. I figured we
were in for it.

"Mom told me about fighting in the pool. I'm disappointed
in both of you. No video games for either of you for a week!" he
exclaimed.

"Aw, jeez," Sean moaned. I looked away. I didn't want to see
Dad's angry face. I felt bad that Sean was getting punished
because I'm the one who caused the fight. Even though it looked
like he was trying to drown me, I never felt like I couldn't get
away. I kept quiet, though.

I kept a low profile the whole week. That was because I had
a plan to ask to go to the zoo on Saturday and I didn't want
Mom to feel I couldn't behave.

"Can we go to the zoo tomorrow?" I asked on Friday.

Mom gave me a stare, then said, "Well, we haven't done that in years. You haven't picked a fight this week. I guess we could give it a try. Dad is not going to work this Saturday."

"Thanks, Mom. I promise I won't pick on Sean," I said.

Ri-g-g-h-t.

CHAPTER THIRTEEN

DAD DROVE us to the zoo. Sean and I talked about our favorite animals, as we were excited to be going to the zoo. Mom and dad stayed quiet in the front of the car.

"I like snow leopards the best," I said. "They are from Asia. They have black spots like other leopards, but the spots are hard to see, and the rest of their fur is white. I think they are beautiful."

"My favorite is the cheetah," said Sean. "It is the fastest mammal. It can run seventy miles per hour."

As I walked into the zoo, I was struck by the strange smells and sounds of all the animals. I didn't remember that from the last time we visited when I was little. There were lots of scents. The strongest of them was something like smelly muck. The zoo was teaming with people and the sun was beating down, but I was too excited to be bothered. The first animals we saw were the gigantic lions. One male growled so loud, I jumped. I jerked my head toward the noise, my eyes popping with surprise. The lion tossed his head and roared again. That was scary. Two lions that looked young were playing, wrestling each other and knocking each other off big rocks.

As we walked, I noticed all the animals had natural looking habitats.

"The animals don't have cages with bars like at other zoos," I commented to Dad.

"No, they don't. Also, many of the animal habitats get rotated now and then to blend the smells and make their environment seem more natural," said Dad.

"You mean they move animals to different parts of the zoo?" I asked as we walked.

"Yeah. They move all the things that are special to each animal, too."

"I'd like to see that happening. But I guess they don't let the public in during those times," I said.

The next exhibit was of zebras. There was a cute baby zebra. The sign said he was one year old and his name was Danzig. Lots of little kids and adults were crowded around him.

All along the way, peacocks walked free. When they made noise, they sounded like they were saying, "Help, help, help." I stared at them. Peacocks have beautiful tail feathers.

"Why do some have great big colorful fan tails and others are just brown?" I asked Dad.

"Well, the ones strutting around with colorful tails are the males. They are showing off for the brown females," he explained.

"Oh. Because they want the girls to like them," I said. Dad laughed.

Throughout the zoo, we could hear the howler monkeys shrieking. We passed a few restaurants with all kinds of food smells coming from them. There was Mexican food, hot dogs, pizza. Our parents walked with Sean and me for a while, and then told us to meet them at a certain bench.

"Come back to the seal display. We'll be here on this bench," said Mom, pointing at a shady spot. "Stay together at all times."

Sean and I watched the seals playing for a bit. One seemed to wave to us. I waved back. It seemed like he was laughing. Then we dashed off.

"I want to see the snow leopards," I said. I had already told Sean they were my favorite.

"Let's go to the cheetahs first," Sean said.

Since I was trying not to start a fight, I agreed to go to the cheetahs first with Sean.

While Sean gazed at the cheetahs, I watched a young boy about six years old throwing peanuts at small animals nearby. There was a sign saying, "Don't feed the animals," but he ignored it. There was a short glass wall around them. One animal, a porcupine, was upset about things being thrown over the wall at him. I saw a picture in my mind of the boy reaching over the wall to touch the porcupine. The animal started throwing quills at the boy.

"Hey, don't do that. You are making him mad," I said to the boy, looking around for the boy's parents. I saw that his mother was tending to a baby lying in a pink carriage, not watching him at all.

"So, what? He can't hurt me," said the boy.

"Yes, he can. He can throw quills at you."

"They can't throw that far," he said.

At that moment, the porcupine bristled and cast off some quills. The mother dashed up, pushing the baby carriage as I pulled the boy out of danger. I'm fast.

"Alan, what are you doing?" shouted the mother. "I told you to not feed the animals." I thought she looked furious.

The mother dragged Alan away without a word to me, pushing the carriage with her other hand and stomping her feet.

I felt sorry for the boy. Sort of. I saw it happen in my mind. It seemed to me that it could happen. I knew I would think about this later, especially as I tried to go to sleep. I would constantly see the porcupine quills flying through the air ready to hit the boy. I wondered what would have happened to him if I hadn't seen the vision. I was still struggling to figure out why and how these things happened in my mind.

"Sean," I said looking to my brother, "I knew the porcupine was going to throw quills at the boy."

"Noah, you're such a weirdo. Things you see in your mind don't happen. Where do you get that stuff?" said Sean.

"Sean, I don't know! I just know I feel like I am popping out of my body sometimes and it is like I see things happening in my mind while I also feel I am floating above myself."

"Like I said, Noah. You are a weirdo," he said, his voice full of scorn.

I felt despair, but I didn't let it show on my face. I decided I wouldn't bother to tell my parents about it. I really need to understand it myself. But how do you understand something no one believes is happening? I know I am having visions. I pop out of my body and I can see what is going to happen to people. I wonder if anyone else has ever had the ability to do this, but they never told anyone because no one would believe them when it started happening. It made me feel better to think there might be someone else like me out there. So I followed Sean to the next cage with animals.

There were cute kangaroos, buffalos, elephants, and two adult polar bears. These bears were going to be shipped off to some place like Alaska or Canada because they wouldn't mate in the zoo. I don't blame them. Who would want to raise their babies in cages?

Sean and I walked on, coming to the habitat for wolves. One wolf sat on a large rock, staring into my eyes. I felt like he was talking to me.

"Do you see how I am, trapped here?" the wolf said. He sounded hopeless.

"I wish I could help," I told him. I felt really bad. I could hear the wolf's voice in my mind. It wasn't like the Harry Potter book when Harry spoke to the snake. No one could hear the wolf because he wasn't making any noise. But I could hear him in my mind. It was like another vision where I'd pop out for a moment then come back.

I felt really bad because I knew I couldn't help him, and I loved visiting the zoo. If there weren't animals in the zoo, there wouldn't be a reason to come to it. I was confused and I wanted to find a way to make the wolf happy, but I didn't know how.

Soon, it was time to meet our parents. We found them still resting in the shade.

"A wolf was telling me how sad he is to be caged," I told Dad when we met them by the seals. "He looked lonely."

I had felt those hopeless wolf eyes touching me in a deep place.

"I don't want to come to the zoo ever again."

"I understand," said Dad. "I don't like seeing animals caged, either. That's why we haven't come in years."

He blew right past me telling him the wolf was talking to me. No one ever understood. I felt despair for me and for the wolf and for all the animals. I wished we had never come. I knew I would always see the eyes of that wolf in my mind. I wouldn't forget. I put my head down so no one would notice I was sad. I didn't want to spoil the fun day for the others.

I couldn't help thinking there was something wrong with me. No one understood what was going on inside my mind. I wondered if I needed to see a doctor to have the visions and dreams removed. Maybe he could give me some vitamins or medicine that would make my mind work like everyone else.

Sean was different, but no one treated him like he was lying. I guess this is where my jealousy comes back. Sean gets all of the attention and I am left alone to figure out what is happening to me.

I'd like to think it is a superpower and one day I'd be able to save people before bad things happen to them, like I was able to do with the boy and the porcupine and the boy at the swimming pool. I just wish people would take notice of me. I wish someone could understand what was happening in my mind. I wish I didn't feel alone.

When we left the zoo, I decided I'd never go back, even to see the snow leopards. I'd have to find a way to free the animals. Maybe when I am older, I can do something about the wolf.

CHAPTER FOURTEEN

SATURDAY ROLLED AROUND. We all were just sitting around. Sean and I were watching cartoons on the television. For once, Dad was not working.

"Would you boys like to go someplace fun today?" Dad asked.

"The Rockies are playing at home this afternoon," I said.

I looked at Sean to see if he thought that sounded good. He nodded, looking excited by the idea.

"Good idea. That would be fun. We'll go to a game," Dad said.

While Dad and I were talking, I saw Mom go into the kitchen. I could smell the chicken cooking and hear the sizzle of grease popping on the stove as she started cooking a lunch of chicken tacos. I got a big smile on my face and rubbed my belly. I couldn't wait for lunch to be ready. Chicken tacos are delicious. My mouth filled with spit as I thought about a large taco sitting on my plate smothered in sauces. I could barely contain my excitement as I waited for Mom to announce lunch was ready.

"Got hot sauce, Mom?" I asked.

I love hot sauce. I would pour the hottest sauce straight down my throat if Mom would let me.

"I bet you are hungry," she said as she fetched the sauce.

"Yeah. I still feel pumped up. I'm starving."

She made extra.

We all went to the Colorado Rockies baseball game. The stadium is much larger on the inside than it looks on the outside. There are 40,000 or 50,000 seats. Everybody was talking. All the sounds together sounded like yelling. There is a huge electric scoreboard. The top of the scoreboard is in the form of the Rocky Mountains and that area is used to display statistics of the baseball players. We got good seats in the shade near the third base line. We watched as the Rockies played the Los Angeles Dodgers. The weather was warm. The stadium smelled like hotdogs, peanuts and beer. I was worried about the loud noise and the crowd of people because I knew if Sean got overstimulated, we might have to leave. It is *always* about Sean. Every time something happened on the field, people jumped around and shouted. I talked to him, explaining the game. Since I play baseball and he doesn't, I figured there was lots he wouldn't understand.

"Hot dogs here," yelled a man every twenty minutes or so. He had a tray around his neck filled with hotdogs, soda, beer, and other treats. He wore jeans, a purple Rockies T-shirt and a paper hat with a purple Coors Field logo on it.

"Can we get a hotdog, Dad?" I asked.

"It's only been a couple of hours since lunch, but sure. You must be getting a growth spurt," Dad said.

I hope.

After five innings, I was stuffed with hotdogs and soda. I thought Sean felt that way too. He gave Ozzie a bite of hotdog. The dog licked his lips before swallowing the piece in one gulp. I wondered if he even tasted it. He wagged his tail and jumped around like he was telling Sean 'thank you.'

Nothing much was happening in the game. I watched as people around us talked and gathered in small groups.

"Do these people know each other?" I asked Dad.

"Probably not really. They just all come to games a lot, so

they see each other around the stadium. They all have baseball to talk about, so they visit with each other," he said.

"Oh. Well, that's one way to make friends, I guess," I said.

Batters on both teams kept striking out. If a Rockies batter got walked, I kept hoping he would steal some bases. That's what I like to do when I play Little League ball. Some of them did that, but never made it to home plate.

Rockies pitcher Tyler Chatwood was throwing a no-hitter game. And Dodgers pitcher Clayton Kershaw had walked a few batters, but no one made it home. There was still no score. Sean started fidgeting. Ozzie laid his head in Sean's lap. Sean started petting Ozzie and calmed down. I was glad that, so far, Sean was not having a fit.

Rockies' right fielder, Carlos Gonzales, came to bat. He is called CarGo. In my mind, I saw him hit a home run over the middle fence. I have my own glove and I thought I could catch that homerun ball if I could walk over where I saw it land.

"Dad, can I move over there?" I asked, pointing to the rows behind midfield.

"No, stay here with us," he said.

"But I think CarGo is going to hit a ball there and I want to catch it."

"Noah, no. I want you to stay with us," he said.

The crowd was chanting "CarGo" over and over. The athlete chalked up two strikes and two balls. On the next pitch, though, he hit the ball out of the park. Everyone jumped up, screaming "CarGo, CarGo" as he ran the bases.

"Did you see that ball fly over the fence? Wow," I yelled.

"Watch CarGo run. He looks like he was born to do it," said Dad.

He had completely forgotten that I asked to go over to where that ball was hit. I get ignored a lot. I felt mad about that but I looked down so he wouldn't see my face. Not that he was looking.

But when the rest of the family sat down, Sean kept jumping

and screaming. Ozzie got his attention. I did too, calming Sean with eye contact. I was sending love but what I really wanted to do was smack Sean. I didn't want us to have to go home because of him. Sean calmed, but Ozzie got the credit. I told my parents how I helped to calm Sean. They didn't believe me.

"I *knew* he was going to hit it," I said to Sean.

"Noah, you did *not* know," said Sean, brushing me off. I wondered if Sean was a little bit jealous of my gift, too, even though he didn't believe me.

I looked away from him so he wouldn't see how hurt I felt. The game ended with the score of 1 - 0. The Rockies won! It took a while to get out of the stadium and out to the car. We had parked far away.

"Whew! I'm tired," said Mom. I saw sweat on her face.

"I know. Me too. Look at the boys though," he replied.

Sean and I were dancing along, running ahead of the adults, then running back again.

"Maybe we should pay the big bucks for closer parking next time," said Mom.

"Yeah, let's remember to do that," said Dad.

When we got in the car, a green Chrysler minivan, it was steaming hot. The seats burned my butt through my jeans. Dad started the car and turned on the air-conditioner. The car had automatic warming seats, but not automatic cooling seats. I wondered if someone would invent cooling seats in the future. I closed my eyes and willed my mind to have a vision, but it didn't work that way. I made a wish that one day seats in cars would have an automatic cooling system for hot days like that one.

CHAPTER FIFTEEN

AT LAST, it was getting close to time for school to be out. The weather was mostly warm. When I went with Sean to take Ozzie for a walk, I noticed the trees were bright green with new leaves. We have a peach tree in the front yard, and it was full of pink flowers. Roses were starting to have tiny buds. Ozzie pulled on the leash, trying to get into the flower bed along our sidewalk. Sean had to pull back to keep him from digging in the loose soil around the plants. This was not normal dirt for our area. Most soil around here is hard clay. But Mom wanted some good loose dirt for her flowers this year, so she ordered a load to be dumped on the front lawn. Dad, Sean, and I spent a Saturday in early spring shoveling the good dirt on top of the flower beds and over the lawn.

"I just want to dig in that dirt. I hear bugs in the ground. I want to play with them," Ozzie said to me in my mind.

I heard him clearly. Sometimes he and I talked like that. If I focused on him, he would make eye contact with me. Then I could hear him. His voice sounded like a boy voice when I heard him in my mind, not like his dog voice when he barked.

"I know, Boy, but Mom would not like that," I thought-said back to him.

I know he heard me in his mind, too, because he wagged his tail and nodded his head. I wondered what I sounded like to him.

The air smelled sweet. I stopped to admire the roses. I could hear them talking to each other, just like with the dog. Their voices were soft like the voices of girls. They sounded happy.

"What are you flowers talking about?" I thought-said to them.

They looked up, startled. I guess no one ever talked to them before.

"We are happy to be making other creatures happy with our pretty faces, sweet smells and nectar for the bees," one big pink rose said in my mind.

I didn't know how I hear these things. I sure couldn't ask anyone. I didn't think this happened to anyone else I knew. They would just make fun of me.

I noticed that Sean and Ozzie were far ahead of me now. Sean turned around.

"What are you doing back there, Noah? You're not smelling the roses again, are you?" he asked in a mocking voice.

"Get over it, Sean. This is what I do. You don't know what you are missing by rushing along, not paying attention to anything," I retorted, walking fast to catch up.

There was going to be a party and continuation ceremony for kids like Sean who were passing from grade school to middle school.

"Are you nervous about the graduation ceremony?" I asked him.

"What's to worry about?" he replied, sounding scornful.

He talked big but I was pretty sure he wasn't looking forward to standing up in front of all the other students and their families and walking across the stage.

"You'll be okay. Ozzie will be with you," I said, wanting to soothe him.

"We should head back. Mom wants us to go shopping for dress up clothes," he said, talking in his bossy voice.

When we got inside, Mom was ready to go shopping.

"Aw, Mom-m-m. Dress up clothes? Shopping? Yuck," I protested.

It did no good.

"Don't even complain, Mister. You know you don't want *me* to pick out your clothes for you. Every time I do that, you don't like what I bring home. So, you can just button up your lip and get in the car," she said.

I knew she was right. I liked to pick out my own clothes. I knew how I wanted to look and she was clueless.

We went to Kohl's Boys Wear. Although I didn't want to be there, it was kind of exciting to walk into the store with all the colors and fresh clothes smells and all the people. My bad mood changed to anticipation as I tore off toward clothes in my size, seven slim. Sean and Ozzie went his own way to the section carrying his size, twelve regular.

"Mom, how about these?" I said, holding up a pair of creased brown khakis. I thought I would look sharp in them.

"That will be fine for you. But I want you to try them on. You might have grown a bit since we bought school clothes," she said.

Under protest, I found the dressing room and tried on the pants. She was right. They were too short and tight.

"Mom, find some size eights for me," I said from behind the dressing room door.

"There you go. See, you have grown," she said as she handed me a pair of size eights.

They fit just right.

As I walked out of the dressing room, she said, "Pick out a button-down dress shirt."

Sean ran up with a pair of khakis too.

"No. I want you to get some dress slacks. You're going to walk across the stage," she told him.

"Aw, Mom, I'll be wearing a long gown. No one will notice."

I giggled at the thought of Sean in a long gown.

"Shut up, Noah," he said.

"Well, okay then. Now get a shirt and tie and I want you and Noah to try on sports coats."

We had dress shoes that we had gotten at Easter that still fit us. We got white shirts, dark blue ties and dark blue blazers. Boring, but Mom approved.

Then we went to a pet shop to see what they had to dress up Ozzie.

"Mom, look at this. They have a shirt that looks like a tuxedo for him. How funny," I said, laughing.

"Yeah, how funny. Here Ozzie. Would you like this?" asked Sean, holding the shirt up to the dog's chest.

Ozzie didn't comment but he danced around, all excited, so I thought he liked it.

After leaving the store, we went to lunch at a pizza place in the mall. I could smell garlic, peppers, and tomato sauce from several stores away. Our pizza arrived, half with pepperoni for me and Mom, half with sausage for Sean. While Mom was gazing at shop windows across the way, I threw a piece of pepperoni at Sean. I couldn't resist.

Sean yelped. "Noah, look at the stain on my shirt. This is my favorite Dale Earnhardt, Jr. shirt."

"I know," I said, giggling.

Sean threw a piece of sausage at me, but I ducked, and the sausage hit Mom, who had turned to scold me just then.

"He started it," said Sean, not wanting to be blamed.

"No, I didn't."

"You did. Look at the grease on my shirt."

Mom looked worn out from dealing with us for hours now. I knew I was in for it. She grabbed both of us, along with the clothing bags, and dragged us out to the car, hissing through clenched teeth the whole way about what brats we were. She completely lost her cool. Even Ozzie cowered as Sean dragged him along. I felt guilty because I had upset Mom, but then there was the satisfaction of picking on Sean.

As Mom drove us home, I began thinking how bad I felt about picking on Sean all the time. I felt bad about upsetting Mom, too. But he hurt my feelings when he called me names because I was different from most people. I didn't know why I heard voices and saw things others don't see. I didn't know what I was supposed to do with the trouble scenes I saw happening in my mind before they actually happened. I'm embarrassed when people make fun of me. Sometimes, my parents looked at me and rolled their eyes. They didn't know what to do about this weird kid of theirs.

At the same time, I was thinking all this, I felt myself pop out of my body. I saw in my mind that if Mom went down this same road, there would be an accident. I saw a big black truck cutting into our lane and smashing into us. I was shocked to see this and popped back in my body, trying to think of what to say to Mom. I knew she wouldn't believe me. I must have made a noise because Mom asked what was wrong.

"Are you okay, Noah? Did I hear you gasp for breath?" she asked, concerned.

"Mom, could we take another way home? How about if we drive past the big horse farm? I like to watch the horses in the pasture."

"I guess we could do that. I like to look at them, too. And we are not in a hurry," she replied.

Whew. Maybe there are ways I can use what I see to avoid bad situations, even if no one believes me.

I didn't have any way of knowing if that accident would really have happened. But I felt relieved I had talked Mom into taking another route.

CHAPTER SIXTEEN

ALL SEMESTER, Mrs. Stein had been teaching the three grades under her supervision about space travel. We were preparing for a field trip to the Challenger Learning Center in Colorado Springs, seventy miles from the school. The name of our mission would be *Return to Mars*. I was excited about the idea we could pretend to go to Mars. Every time she talked about it; my imagination ran with images of what it might be like to land on Mars.

We sat in a big circle when she wanted to talk to all of us at once.

"Isn't Mars supposed to be really hot?" I asked.

"Actually, no. The average temperature is about 65 degrees. It does get much hotter at the equator, but also way below freezing at the poles. It looks hot, though, because it is red and we always see pictures of the sun blazing and dust in the air," she responded.

She explained to all the classes, "The Challenger Learning Center was developed by surviving family members of the seven astronauts who died in a fiery explosion of the *Challenger* Space Shuttle in 1986, long before you were even born."

"What happened to cause the explosion?" I asked.

"Noah, you always want to know everything," Sean

complained. He seemed grouchy this day. Maybe he hadn't slept well the night before.

"Something went wrong with one of the parts, the O ring," Mrs. Stein replied, ignoring Sean. "The metal O ring was already damaged when it was put in place, but no one noticed. There were five astronauts and two civilians on board. One of the civilians was a schoolteacher named Christa McAuliffe."

She pulled down the white screen at the front of the classroom and showed us a video of the explosion. There were hundreds of people gathered near the launch pad to watch. There was a huge noise as the ship started going up into the deep blue sky. Then it flew apart with horrible, exploding sounds. A bunch of smoke poured into the sky as parts of the ship flew in all directions at once. The crowd started screaming and so did everyone in class. We were watching seven brave people die. An announcer was talking from the Houston Control Center, and he just was saying normal things. He was not even watching what was actually happening in those first seconds. Then we heard him scream, "Oh, my God!" Then there was more screaming in the control center.

"How awful!" I exclaimed, my eyes bugging out. I turned to see Leah wiping tears from her eyes. Everyone in the circle was shocked by the explosion.

"Yes. Christa taught fifth grade. She wanted to go on the flight so she could come back to her classroom and teach her students about space travel," Mrs. Stein said, her voice full of sorrow. She looked sad, too.

"Like you," said Brian. His voice sounded stunned, like I felt.

"Yes. And the families wanted to honor their people who died by creating a center where students can learn all about traveling in outer space. The mission we will participate in at the Challenger Center will be a trip to Mars."

"How far away is Mars?" I asked.

"It takes seven months to get there in real time," she replied. "We will pretend we are almost there."

We studied all kinds of things like problem solving in situations where something went wrong, weather on Mars, the importance of communication, and working as a team. I was thinking the first problem of all would be how to grow food on Mars.

"Mrs. Stein, is there water on Mars?"

"Yes, Noah. Scientists have now discovered water there. Most of it is in the form of ice, but using robots, they have been able to access the salty water and use it to grow food."

"Oh, that's a relief," I said.

"They have also found fish fossils. That means that at one time, there were fish in the water. Another feature recently analyzed is the presence of small blue rocks. They look like blueberries because of the color and shape. Similar rocks are found in Utah."

"What causes the blue rocks to form?" I asked.

Sean rolled his eyes at me. I knew he was thinking I was a nosy person.

"The blueberries, as they are being called, are formed when water that contains a lot of iron seeps through bedrock," she replied.

While she continued talking, my mind was bursting with the possibilities of all that.

"Mars has huge red dust storms that last a long time. One storm can almost cover the whole planet. You will get lots of information on the locations of dust storms during the mission. You will have to land the spaceship in a place where there is no storm," she said.

This sounded exciting to me.

There would be nine jobs for students on a simulated flight to a space station and beyond to the moon, she told us. As we learned, each student tested to determine for which job they would be best suited. I was thrilled with the idea of space flight. For me, communication from Mission Control to the spaceship seemed most important and I tested to be in that role. Sean wanted to be an astronaut on the spaceship.

The next day, Leah was not in school, or the day after that. I called her when I got home.

"Are you okay?" I asked.

"I am okay now, but it upset me to watch the *Challenger* blow up. I've been having nightmares about it," she said.

"Oh, no! Leah, that happened a long time ago, before we were even born," I said.

"I know, but it really upset me to see it for real. My mom called Mrs. Stein and raised heck with her about showing that film," she said.

"Oh. I wondered why Mrs. Stein seemed upset. Gosh, Leah. What do you think is going to happen?"

"I don't know. Mrs. Stein came over and talked to my parents. She apologized a lot. I don't think Mom wants me to go on the field trip. She might not even let me go to the same school next year."

"Leah, I would miss you so much. You're my best friend."

"I would miss you too. We'll just have to see what happens."

I got off the phone feeling sad. That evening, as I thought about Leah not coming to our school next year, I popped out of my body. I saw in my mind that Leah was working on school stuff at home. I thought it meant she would be homeschooled now. I went back into the present time. I thought I wouldn't see her again this year and I was even more sad.

CHAPTER SEVENTEEN

AT LAST, the day of the field trip arrived. Leah was not in class again. The weather was warm as we loaded into a white school van. I was glad the van was air-conditioned. Mrs. Stein and Miss Millhone rode with us students in the bus. The other fourth, fifth, and sixth grade classes, along with their teachers, were in separate buses.

As we rode across Denver and past a few small towns to the Learning Center, there was a lot of excited chatter. I sat across the aisle from the teachers so I could ask questions about space. I really do want to know everything.

"What makes Mars look red?" I asked.

"Remember, we talked about this in class," Mrs. Stein said.

"Oh, yeah. The soil has a high content of iron that gives it the color," I remembered.

"Tell me again what our mission will be?" I asked, feeling excitement bubbling in me.

"You must be feeling anxious about all this. Your mind is jumping all over the place. Remember, part of the class will be on the spaceship, taking supplies to the Mars station already there. The other part of the class will pretend to be astronauts already at the Mars Base One camp, ready to receive needed supplies. Got it?" Mrs. Stein said.

"Oh, yeah. I guess I am feeling anxious. Mostly, though, I'm worried about Leah. Do you think her parents will take her out of school?"

"I talked with them. I wanted to talk to her, too, but they wouldn't allow it. They were afraid she would get more upset. I'm so sorry to have upset her. I'm not sure what they will do now," she said.

"Do you think people on Mars might pollute it with alien bacteria?" I wondered.

"Noah, that is something scientists are looking at. They don't have answers yet," she said.

Also, I love to read all the road signs along the way of any trip. As we got close to Colorado Springs, I noticed several exits off the freeway to explore a national park.

"What is Garden of the Gods?" I asked Mrs. Stein.

"That is a huge formation of red sandstone rock that was formed about a billion years ago," she replied.

"Why is it called that?"

"Well, ancient peoples thought the shapes of the towering rocks looked like ancient gods gathered together."

I stared at formations visible from the road. I felt myself pop out of my body. In my mind, I could see ancient Indians standing together, talking about how there wasn't enough game to feed the tribe anymore, about how they might have to move away. I saw a woman sitting by a campfire. She gazed off at a group of men meeting across the way. One looked up at her with a longing gaze. It seemed he wanted to be with her, but he couldn't. He had to go with the other men to hunt for food.

"Noah, are you okay?" Mrs. Stein spoke to me, popping me back in my body.

"Yeah. I was just thinking about how life must have been for the Native Americans a long time ago," I said. I didn't want to tell her I saw things happening in my mind. I was already teased by some of the kids in class about being a weirdo all the time. "How did the rocks get like that?"

"The earth was in turmoil for millions of years before mountains settled into shapes we see now. This area was formed by an upheaval along a fault line. You know what a fault line is?"

"Yeah. Where the earth has giant cracks that shift."

"That's close enough. There are fossils that show lots of dinosaurs and sea creatures lived here."

"And people lived here not so long ago," I said.

"Yes. There are petroglyphs that tell stories of human life here. Those are picture carvings in rocks made by ancient people who did not have written language yet."

"Wow. I'd like to explore the Garden of the Gods."

"Maybe that could be a field trip for next year," responded Mrs. Stein.

As the van rolled closer to the Learning Center, a storm developed from the East. Suddenly, there was thunder, lightning, and rain pounding on the roof of the van. In my mind, I remembered the last lightning and thunderstorm that took the electricity out at my house and caused a tree to fall in the yard. I wondered if something would happen, but a vision didn't occur.

CHAPTER EIGHTEEN

AS OUR VAN approached the Challenger Learning Center, I was impressed with how the angular building looked like something from the future. Employees brought wet gear out to the van and we dashed through the pouring rain to get inside. Still, my black tennis shoes filled with water, so I was squishy for a while. On the walls of the cool-looking indoors, I saw posters from various space events, including the *Challenger* disaster. I wanted to stop to read all the information on them.

"Can I stay in here and read the posters?" I asked Mrs. Stein.

"I know how much you want to know *everything*. But we have to complete our mission first," she said, chuckling.

We were hustled into a room by our guide, a commander. The room was designed to look like a NASA mission control center. Everything looked like metal. There were computer stations everywhere, and some kind of box we were told would simulate how it would feel if we had no gravity. I thought that sounded like fun.

"Can I get into the simulator?" I asked the commander.

"Sure. When you complete your mission, you can take turns with your classmates," he replied.

The instructor, Commander Magie, guided each of us to our

job locations. He told us what to expect. He said Orion, the spacecraft, had picked up a load of supplies from the International Space Station to transport to Mars.

"We are going to pretend the year is 2076. There is already a habitat set up on Mars. The purpose of our mission is to bring supplies to the astronauts already on Mars," Commander Magie instructed.

"Sir, my shoes are still wet. I've heard that if I am wet and I touch electric stuff, I could get shocked." I said to him.

"That won't happen here. Everything is grounded," he said, smiling.

Each of us was given a white lab coat with a space traveler patch on it to wear. Half of us went to the Mission Control center, including me. The other half, including Sean, boarded a simulated Orion spacecraft.

After a simulated noisy liftoff of the Orion spacecraft, communications between Mission Control, called Mars Base 1, and those on the ship became super important. Also, there were reports from a Rover on Mars about weather details.

"There is a huge dust storm flowing in from the East. You'll only have one hour to unload your cargo before you need to be indoors," warned a commanding voice coming from the Rover.

Each of us had a script for our job. My job was to sit at the communications post and report important details between Mission Control and the spacecraft. Much detailed information passed between Mission Control and the spaceship. We were almost at the end of the mission when a problem developed.

"From Mission Control to the spacecraft." I made my voice sound urgent and announced. "We've detected a decrease in the bio-humidity of the craft. All crew members are instructed to touch the black bar along the left side of your craft in case of an emergency. Repeat: There has been a decrease in the humidity in your environment. Do not touch any other metal gear. This would cause an electrical shock. All crew members are instructed to grasp and hold the black bar covered along the left side of your craft!"

The student astronauts, including Sean, rushed to grab the black bar and held on a few moments.

"Mission Control to the spacecraft, I said in a commanding voice, the electricity has been discharged. You are safe to return to work."

I could hear exclamations of relief from the spacecraft along with chatter and nervous laughter.

"That was a blast," I said to Commander Magie.

"All of you did good work. If you had not communicated right, we would have had to scrub the mission of Orion and that crew would have to return to Earth," said the commander.

After our mission was complete, we moved to the zero gravity simulators. I waited impatiently as I watched my class-mates enter one at a time and experience what it was like to go into space. When it was finally my turn, I suddenly felt a bit nervous. I'd never experienced zero gravity.

As I entered the simulator, I waited until it started and suddenly my body flew up in the air. I flipped in circles and floated around the simulator. It felt strange, and I wanted to puke. When I exited the simulator, I sat on the ground hoping my head would stop turning. I felt dizzy.

Soon everyone had finished the simulators, and it was time to go back to the van. Sean and I and the rest of our class chattered about the experience all the way home.

"That feeling of no gravity was really weird!" I said. I wondered if everyone felt sick like I had during the simulator.

"Yeah, I think if you had no gravity for very long, all your food would come up," said Sean.

"Wow. That's exactly how I felt," I said.

"But astronauts wear special equipment that helps them feel grounded like on Earth, I think," said Brian. I looked at Brian and closed my eyes. He still had the red C on his shirt. What could it mean? Why was it still there? I tried to avoid looking at him so I wouldn't see the red C. But it was always there.

"Gosh, I hope so," I said.

It felt good to have a day free of visions. I didn't have to worry about not being believed. I didn't have to watch for someone getting hurt. I spent the day being a normal kid, just like all of my friends and Sean. It felt good.

your life. I like to get on the minibike with a screen that shows my heart rate. I played around with it, watching how my heart rate changed as I went from slow to fast on the bike.

There's another exhibit where you can learn about space travel. And a platform where you can stand and look out over all of Denver. There was a brown cloud of pollution over the city this day, so not much to see. Another exhibit is a place where you can watch paleontologists work on bones. The school brought in lunch for everyone, but you could go to the museum cafeteria if you wanted. We stayed about four hours.

As we rode back to the school in the van, I had more questions for Mrs. Stein.

"What do you think happened to all the dinosaurs?" I asked.

"Noah, you are so funny. You want to know *everything*," she said.

"Yes. I really always want to know everything. What do you think happened to them?"

"I thought you might ask. There are lots of theories out there. One of them states that sixty-six million years ago there was an asteroid the size of a mountain that hit Mexico. It was going about 40,000 miles per hour. It set off a chain of events that wiped out eighty percent of all life on Earth, including the dinosaurs," she replied.

"I'd like to know more about what that was like," I said.

"How about if you do a research paper on what happened to the dinosaurs? Is there a computer at home that you can use?" she asked.

"Sean has his own computer, but I don't. Mom would let me use hers, I think," I replied.

"Do you think you could work on that tonight?" she asked.

"I think I could. I really want to know more," I said.

"You could turn it in on Thursday. You can even read it in front of the class, if you want. I will give you extra credit for a good paper," she said.

That sounded good to me. My grades could use a boost.

CHAPTER NINETEEN

THE LAST DAY of school had almost arrived. Our class plus the other class of the same age students went on another field trip. This time, we went to the Denver Museum. There was a huge glass front door, but classes went through a side door. There was a ticket counter, a gift shop, and escalators for school kids. There was a place where you could leave your stuff like backpacks.

"What are we going to explore?" I asked Mrs. Stein.

"We teachers know all you students love to study dinosaurs. We'll go to those rooms today."

Two teachers and four parents herded twelve children around the displays. Sean was walking in front of me. We came to a table that had a lot of plastic bits of bone that looked fossilized on it. I grabbed a small bone about eight inches long off a table and smacked Sean on the back of the head, then quickly put the bone back in place.

"Noah," Sean protested in a harsh, low tone.

"What?" I snickered behind my hand.

Sean fumed because, again, I got away with pestering him. I knew Sean wouldn't retaliate in a place like the museum.

Once again, I found a way to vent the jealousy I felt toward Brainiac Sean.

Right away, we saw the enormous Tyrannosaurus Rex, called T. rex for short. It is called the king of dinosaurs because at the time the skeleton was discovered, it was the largest one known. It weighed about nine tons and was about forty feet long. I like T. rex the best of all the dinosaurs. I was thinking about when I saw it in that scary movie, *Jurassic Park*.

"Mrs. Stein, do you think the kind of thing pictured in the Jurassic Park movie could really happen?" I asked.

"That is something to think about. I don't know for sure. But if humans can think how to do it, I guess it *could* happen. I don't think such a thing *will* happen, though. Nothing to worry about, Noah," she said, patting my back.

"Look at those tiny arms," said Brian, still with a big red 'C' on his shirt. I still didn't understand why I could see it.

"Yeah, it would not even have been able to reach its mouth," I said.

"That's why its head and mouth are so big. It could just snap the head off another animal with its huge jaws," said Sean.

Smarty-pants.

When we got to the new part of the exhibit, there was a short dinosaur called the Euroraptor. It was only about three feet tall, shorter than me.

"What would such a short dinosaur eat?" I asked Mrs. Stein.

"They likely ate worms and lizards. They also ate animals that were already dead. They were scavengers," she replied.

Somehow, while I was standing in front of the Euroraptor, I popped out of my body. I felt like I was walking along with the Euroraptor, looking for food. I didn't see me there. I felt me there. I know humans were not on Earth during the dinosaur era. But somehow, I could see, hear, and smell all the sounds of some kind of jungle. And I could see and hear the Euroraptor. And I could feel him. He was hungry, but wary of getting in the way of larger dinosaurs that might eat him. The air was dense

and felt wet, swampy. A big dinosaur spotted the Euroraptor and began to chase him. The Euroraptor screamed as the big guy clamped down on his back. At that moment, I felt a hand clap down on *my* back! It was Sean.

"Noah, you are falling behind," he said.

I jumped and looked at him, startled. I saw I was the only one in the class still standing near the Euroraptor.

"What were you doing? Daydreaming again?" Sean asked.

"I wasn't daydreaming. I was really there with the dinosaurs," I said.

"Noah, you were not. What a weirdo!" Sean exclaimed.

But I was. The dinosaurs were alive. I wonder if they could still be around, just in another dimension and time; not on Earth or in Earth time. Sean was right. I was a weirdo. But I'd seen movies about time travel, like *Back to the Future*. And I'd also see movies about life in other dimensions, like some of the *Star Tr* stuff. If people can think of it, it can happen. I hurried to ca up with the class.

They were standing before a huge animal called the G tosaurus. It was even bigger than T. rex. The information said it was longer than T. rex and weighed about fourteen to

We also saw a Suchomimus that was about twelve feet was found in the Sahara Desert in Africa. Mrs. Stein sa fish.

"Did the Sahara Desert used to be under water?" I a

"Yes. Millions of years ago, it was part of an oc Stein replied.

Another dinosaur that I recognized from the movie was the Stegosaurus. It was found in Col plants, but there were no flowers during this time years ago. It had big bony plates down its back and

Kids can go into other parts of the museum like to go to the Expedition Health section. He into different machines that tell you about y shows you what you would look like at age 75 was so cute in his own tuxedo. He wagged his tail and looked at me in the audience. I could hear him thinking.

"This is fun," he said in my head.

"Yeah, it is. Something different," I thought-said to him.

"I need to pee," he said.

"Hold onto it, boy. I'll tell Sean to take you out in a few minutes," I said to him.

Sean accepted congratulations from the administrative staff of the school, as well as an award for being a straight A student.

I knew I shouldn't feel jealous because in two years, it would be my turn. But I did. As soon as Sean got back to the audience, I told him we should take Ozzie out for a pee break. He agreed.

At the school-wide party that followed, I admired the gym that was decorated in purple and white streamers and balloons with signs of congratulations to the sixth graders all around. There was a punch bowl and baked treats on a table. Loud dance music played. A song by Ariana Grande was playing.

Dressed up in my new clothes, I chatted it up with all my friends, including Leah.

"Would you like to dance with me?" she asked.

I was surprised and I kind of stumbled when I tried to speak.

"Well, yeah. We could do that," I finally stammered.

We held hands as we walked onto the dance floor. I didn't know how to dance, really, but I kind of watched older kids and imitated them. With Leah dancing in front of me, I felt kind of lucy, somehow. I'm glad it was a fast song. I don't know what I would I have done if it had been a slow song.

I saw that Sean, who had put his cap and gown in the car, was standing off by himself. Sean doesn't like this kind of thing. I noticed Mom, a parent helper, walking up to Sean.

"How are you doing, Sean?" I heard Mom ask. She knew the noise and lights were not good for him. I watched him because an early warning sign that Sean was beginning to flip out was that his eyes looked kind of freaky like in those old movies about people being hypnotized and their eyes look dazed. I don't think

Soon, it was time to go home.

As I ran into the house, I saw my mom and immediately thought about the extra credit assignment. "Hi Mom. Can I use your computer? Mrs. Stein asked me to do a research paper on what happened to the dinosaurs for extra credit," I asked.

"Well, sure. How about we start looking at information after dinner?" she said.

I couldn't wait for dinner to be over so I could jump on Mom's computer. I wanted to know two things. I wondered what caused the extinction of dinosaurs, and also what happened to create the Sahara Desert in Africa, a place where many dinosaur fossils are found. There's tons of websites that talk about what happened to dinosaurs. But still, nobody really knows. The two big thoughts are that they were killed off by the impact of an asteroid in Mexico or they were killed by toxic gas from a huge volcanic eruption. The Sahara Desert was once a lush, green oasis where dinosaurs and many creatures found food and water. The theory is that climate change caused the desert we see today.

By Thursday I had a lot of research and was able to share it with the class. I had fun reading my paper to the class. For once, I was the smarty-pants.

CHAPTER TWENTY

FRIDAY EVENING WAS the continuation ceremony. There were only twelve students moving on to middle school this year, so I thought it would not take long. The first thing that happened was that some older Boy Scouts marched in carrying the flags of the United States and Colorado.

"Why are Boy Scouts carrying the flags?" I asked Dad.

"They are probably working on getting their Eagle Scout badges. Community service is part of the requirements," he said.

"Cause before I've seen old guys marching with the flags. I've seen them in parades, I think. Who are *those* guys?" I asked Dad.

"They are with the local post for Veterans of Foreign Wars," Dad said.

"You mean they fought in wars from a long time ago?"

"And some not so long ago. Remember, we are at war in Afghanistan now. We have been for seventeen years," he said.

"But these guys look old," I said.

"Yes. They look like they were probably in Korea or Vietnam. Many years before you were born," he said.

"Why do people keep having wars?" I asked.

"Well, some have religious beliefs that they want everyone in their country to practice. When people resist, war can begin.

"Other times, there is a person who wants to take o a country, so he starts a war to make the people do way. There are lots of reasons," he said.

"I don't see what difference it makes if not believes the same way I do. And how can anyone thinl rule a country by killing off all the people who don't them? That sounds dumb," I said.

Dad didn't respond. He was used to me asl everything.

One of the Boy Scouts was commanding the othe stop and when to go and when to turn, I think, base the guys were doing. He used some kind of words I r before, or at least, I couldn't understand them t pronounced them.

Someone announced that a high school stud Fisher, would sing the national anthem. She v because she was on *American Idol*. Mom really likes and Sean and I usually watch it with her. D sometimes.

We all stood and put hands across our hearts as t dark-haired girl sang, "Oh say, can you see, by the light" and the rest of it.

"I can't believe she can sing such high notes," to Dad.

"It is a difficult song. But be quiet and listen," he Then we sat down.

Recorded music was playing a song I've heard a ation ceremonies, like when my cousin, Charlot high school.

"Mom, what is that song called?" I asked.

"The title is 'Pomp and Circumstance,'" she sai

"It sounds like you could march to it," I said.

"Yes. That is what you will see happening no the twelve graduates started walking into the audit

Sean and Ozzie walked across the stage in ful

CHAPTER TWENTY

FRIDAY EVENING WAS the continuation ceremony. There were only twelve students moving on to middle school this year, so I thought it would not take long. The first thing that happened was that some older Boy Scouts marched in carrying the flags of the United States and Colorado.

"Why are Boy Scouts carrying the flags?" I asked Dad.

"They are probably working on getting their Eagle Scout badges. Community service is part of the requirements," he said.

"Cause before I've seen old guys marching with the flags. I've seen them in parades, I think. Who are *those* guys?" I asked Dad.

"They are with the local post for Veterans of Foreign Wars," Dad said.

"You mean they fought in wars from a long time ago?"

"And some not so long ago. Remember, we are at war in Afghanistan now. We have been for seventeen years," he said.

"But these guys look old," I said.

"Yes. They look like they were probably in Korea or Vietnam. Many years before you were born," he said.

"Why do people keep having wars?" I asked.

"Well, some have religious beliefs that they want everyone in their country to practice. When people resist, war can begin.

Soon, it was time to go home.

As I ran into the house, I saw my mom and immediately thought about the extra credit assignment. "Hi Mom. Can I use your computer? Mrs. Stein asked me to do a research paper on what happened to the dinosaurs for extra credit," I asked.

"Well, sure. How about we start looking at information after dinner?" she said.

I couldn't wait for dinner to be over so I could jump on Mom's computer. I wanted to know two things. I wondered what caused the extinction of dinosaurs, and also what happened to create the Sahara Desert in Africa, a place where many dinosaur fossils are found. There's tons of websites that talk about what happened to dinosaurs. But still, nobody really knows. The two big thoughts are that they were killed off by the impact of an asteroid in Mexico or they were killed by toxic gas from a huge volcanic eruption. The Sahara Desert was once a lush, green oasis where dinosaurs and many creatures found food and water. The theory is that climate change caused the desert we see today.

By Thursday I had a lot of research and was able to share it with the class. I had fun reading my paper to the class. For once, I was the smarty-pants.

your life. I like to get on the minibike with a screen that shows my heart rate. I played around with it, watching how my heart rate changed as I went from slow to fast on the bike.

There's another exhibit where you can learn about space travel. And a platform where you can stand and look out over all of Denver. There was a brown cloud of pollution over the city this day, so not much to see. Another exhibit is a place where you can watch paleontologists work on bones. The school brought in lunch for everyone, but you could go to the museum cafeteria if you wanted. We stayed about four hours.

As we rode back to the school in the van, I had more questions for Mrs. Stein.

"What do you think happened to all the dinosaurs?" I asked.

"Noah, you are so funny. You want to know *everything*," she said.

"Yes. I really always want to know everything. What do you think happened to them?"

"I thought you might ask. There are lots of theories out there. One of them states that sixty-six million years ago there was an asteroid the size of a mountain that hit Mexico. It was going about 40,000 miles per hour. It set off a chain of events that wiped out eighty percent of all life on Earth, including the dinosaurs," she replied.

"I'd like to know more about what that was like," I said.

"How about if you do a research paper on what happened to the dinosaurs? Is there a computer at home that you can use?" she asked.

"Sean has his own computer, but I don't. Mom would let me use hers, I think," I replied.

"Do you think you could work on that tonight?" she asked.

"I think I could. I really want to know more," I said.

"You could turn it in on Thursday. You can even read it in front of the class, if you want. I will give you extra credit for a good paper," she said.

That sounded good to me. My grades could use a boost.

and felt wet, swampy. A big dinosaur spotted the Euroraptor and began to chase him. The Euroraptor screamed as the big guy clamped down on his back. At that moment, I felt a hand clap down on *my* back! It was Sean.

"Noah, you are falling behind," he said.

I jumped and looked at him, startled. I saw I was the only one in the class still standing near the Euroraptor.

"What were you doing? Daydreaming again?" Sean asked.

"I wasn't daydreaming. I was really there with the dinosaurs," I said.

"Noah, you were not. What a weirdo!" Sean exclaimed.

But I was. The dinosaurs were alive. I wonder if they could still be around, just in another dimension and time; not on Earth or in Earth time. Sean was right. I was a weirdo. But I'd seen movies about time travel, like *Back to the Future*. And I'd also seen movies about life in other dimensions, like some of the *Star Trek* stuff. If people can think of it, it can happen. I hurried to catch up with the class.

They were standing before a huge animal called the Gigantosaurus. It was even bigger than T. rex. The information sign said it was longer than T. rex and weighed about fourteen tons.

We also saw a Suchomimus that was about twelve feet tall. It was found in the Sahara Desert in Africa. Mrs. Stein said it ate fish.

"Did the Sahara Desert used to be under water?" I asked.

"Yes. Millions of years ago, it was part of an ocean," Mrs. Stein replied.

Another dinosaur that I recognized from the *Jurassic Park* movie was the Stegosaurus. It was found in Colorado. It ate plants, but there were no flowers during this time of 160 million years ago. It had big bony plates down its back and tail.

Kids can go into other parts of the museum, too, I knew. I like to go to the Expedition Health section. Here you can plug into different machines that tell you about your health. One shows you what you would look like at age 75 if you smoked all

Once again, I found a way to vent the jealousy I felt toward Brainiac Sean.

Right away, we saw the enormous Tyrannosaurus Rex, called T. rex for short. It is called the king of dinosaurs because at the time the skeleton was discovered, it was the largest one known. It weighed about nine tons and was about forty feet long. I like T. rex the best of all the dinosaurs. I was thinking about when I saw it in that scary movie, *Jurassic Park*.

"Mrs. Stein, do you think the kind of thing pictured in the Jurassic Park movie could really happen?" I asked.

"That is something to think about. I don't know for sure. But if humans can think how to do it, I guess it *could* happen. I don't think such a thing *will* happen, though. Nothing to worry about, Noah," she said, patting my back.

"Look at those tiny arms," said Brian, still with a big red 'C' on his shirt. I still didn't understand why I could see it.

"Yeah, it would not even have been able to reach its mouth," I said.

"That's why its head and mouth are so big. It could just snap the head off another animal with its huge jaws," said Sean.

Smarty-pants.

When we got to the new part of the exhibit, there was a short dinosaur called the Euroraptor. It was only about three feet tall, shorter than me.

"What would such a short dinosaur eat?" I asked Mrs. Stein.

"They likely ate worms and lizards. They also ate animals that were already dead. They were scavengers," she replied.

Somehow, while I was standing in front of the Euroraptor, I popped out of my body. I felt like I was walking along with the Euroraptor, looking for food. I didn't see me there. I felt me there. I know humans were not on Earth during the dinosaur era. But somehow, I could see, hear, and smell all the sounds of some kind of jungle. And I could see and hear the Euroraptor. And I could feel him. He was hungry, but wary of getting in the way of larger dinosaurs that might eat him. The air was dense

CHAPTER NINETEEN

THE LAST DAY of school had almost arrived. Our class plus the other class of the same age students went on another field trip. This time, we went to the Denver Museum. There was a huge glass front door, but classes went through a side door. There was a ticket counter, a gift shop, and escalators for school kids. There was a place where you could leave your stuff like backpacks.

"What are we going to explore?" I asked Mrs. Stein.

"We teachers know all you students love to study dinosaurs. We'll go to those rooms today."

Two teachers and four parents herded twelve children around the displays. Sean was walking in front of me. We came to a table that had a lot of plastic bits of bone that looked fossilized on it. I grabbed a small bone about eight inches long off a table and smacked Sean on the back of the head, then quickly put the bone back in place.

"Noah," Sean protested in a harsh, low tone.

"What?" I snickered behind my hand.

Sean fumed because, again, I got away with pestering him. I knew Sean wouldn't retaliate in a place like the museum.

was so cute in his own tuxedo. He wagged his tail and looked at me in the audience. I could hear him thinking.

"This is fun," he said in my head.

"Yeah, it is. Something different," I thought-said to him.

"I need to pee," he said.

"Hold onto it, boy. I'll tell Sean to take you out in a few minutes," I said to him.

Sean accepted congratulations from the administrative staff of the school, as well as an award for being a straight A student.

I knew I shouldn't feel jealous because in two years, it would be my turn. But I did. As soon as Sean got back to the audience, I told him we should take Ozzie out for a pee break. He agreed.

At the school-wide party that followed, I admired the gym that was decorated in purple and white streamers and balloons with signs of congratulations to the sixth graders all around. There was a punch bowl and baked treats on a table. Loud dance music played. A song by Ariana Grande was playing.

Dressed up in my new clothes, I chatted it up with all my friends, including Leah.

"Would you like to dance with me?" she asked.

I was surprised and I kind of stumbled when I tried to speak.

"Well, yeah. We could do that," I finally stammered.

We held hands as we walked onto the dance floor. I didn't know how to dance, really, but I kind of watched older kids and imitated them. With Leah dancing in front of me, I felt kind of juicy, somehow. I'm glad it was a fast song. I don't know what I would I have done if it had been a slow song.

I saw that Sean, who had put his cap and gown in the car, was standing off by himself. Sean doesn't like this kind of thing. I noticed Mom, a parent helper, walking up to Sean.

"How are you doing, Sean?" I heard Mom ask. She knew the noise and lights were not good for him. I watched him because an early warning sign that Sean was beginning to flip out was that his eyes looked kind of freaky like in those old movies about people being hypnotized and their eyes look dazed. I don't think

"Other times, there is a person who wants to take over ruling a country, so he starts a war to make the people do things his way. There are lots of reasons," he said.

"I don't see what difference it makes if not everybody believes the same way I do. And how can anyone think they can rule a country by killing off all the people who don't agree with them? That sounds dumb," I said.

Dad didn't respond. He was used to me asking 'why' everything.

One of the Boy Scouts was commanding the others when to stop and when to go and when to turn, I think, based on what the guys were doing. He used some kind of words I never heard before, or at least, I couldn't understand them the way he pronounced them.

Someone announced that a high school student, Alisha Fisher, would sing the national anthem. She was famous because she was on *American Idol*. Mom really likes to watch it and Sean and I usually watch it with her. Dad watches sometimes.

We all stood and put hands across our hearts as this beautiful dark-haired girl sang, "Oh say, can you see, by the dawn's early light" and the rest of it.

"I can't believe she can sing such high notes," I whispered to Dad.

"It is a difficult song. But be quiet and listen," he replied.

Then we sat down.

Recorded music was playing a song I've heard at other graduation ceremonies, like when my cousin, Charlotte, graduated high school.

"Mom, what is that song called?" I asked.

"The title is 'Pomp and Circumstance,'" she said.

"It sounds like you could march to it," I said.

"Yes. That is what you will see happening now," she said, as the twelve graduates started walking into the auditorium.

Sean and Ozzie walked across the stage in full regalia. Ozzie that's what really happens during hypnosis, though. Maybe I'd like to be hypnotized sometime.

"Noah always has girlfriends. I've never had even one," said Sean with a pout.

"Look at that pretty girl. She is giving you the eye, Sean. Go ask her to dance," Mom suggested.

"Mom, I don't know how to dance," he replied.

"Neither does Noah, but he was just doing what he saw other kids doing. Give it a try," she encouraged.

"I'd rather just watch," he said.

"Well, okay. But don't complain that you don't have a girlfriend," Mom said.

I felt bad for Sean. I know he has a hard time speaking to people. It's like his tongue gets tied. You can see him thinking hard about how to say what is in his mind.

I also felt smirky.

CHAPTER TWENTY-ONE

THE NEXT DAY, Sean and I asked to go to the Elitch's Garden Theme and Water Park to celebrate the end of school.

"Do you want to invite some friends?" Mom asked.

"Mom, we don't have real friends. Noah has friends at school, but they are not real," Sean said.

That wasn't true. Brian was a real friend. So was Leah. But I just kept my mouth shut. If we invited friends and Sean went into a tizzy with all the crowds and noise, we all would have to go home. I'd be embarrassed.

"Why not?" Mom asked.

"Because I have a hard time making friends and some of the kids think Noah is weird," Sean explained.

I did know that she already knew these things. I thought she just brought it up, hoping for a clue as to how to help us.

I was aware our parents used to worry about taking Sean to a place like Elitch's Garden with so much noise, lights and people, but since Ozzie came into our lives to help keep him calm, they felt they could allow both of us this kind of fun. I got that we could do more things with the help of the dog. Still, it was all about Sean and I felt alone.

We had special passes at the park that allowed us to run to the front of the line to buy tickets. We knew our parents expected us to come back to a specified pavilion in two hours. We always took off running as soon as we got in the gates, but we knew where we were supposed to meet them, always the same place. The morning was still cool, but I knew that would change in an hour or so. The park smelled sweet like cotton candy, salty like peanuts, and sweaty from bodies. There was always loud noise from the clanging of the rides and screams of people on them. You could always tell when screaming was going to happen if you watched the rides. Screaming happened after the chairs reached the top and started down the other side, like with Mind Eraser, my favorite ride, a red flashing coaster that suspended riders and blasted them through rollovers, dives, and spins. When you heard it go up the first loop, you automatically listened for a multitude of screams. And there were brilliant lights everywhere.

I ran to the Mind Eraser. I did not eat much at breakfast. I didn't want to barf. There was a long line, like always, but thanks to my special ticket, I dashed to the front of the line.

I watched Sean and Ozzie take off in another direction. I knew Sean's favorite ride was the Star Flyer, an extreme swing ride. Ozzie could not follow Sean onto the rides, but he was well trained to sit patiently at the base of a ride while Sean flew through the sky.

I knew Mom and Dad were sitting in the pavilion, having a little relaxation time to themselves. I thought that was a good thing.

In no time, I was on the monster coaster, blasting through rollovers, dives, and double corkscrew spins. Yeah, good thing I didn't eat much breakfast.

After all that, I felt like something a little quieter would be good. I went to the Dragonwing. I had to stand at the height measuring spot, but I already knew this was the first year I was tall enough not to need a parent with me. I didn't know what was such a big deal. Maybe if you were too short, you could accidentally slide under the safety bar. I climbed into a seat with black dragon wings on each side. Off we went, flying around with dragons. I thought I was really flying with a dragon for a minute or two.

Two hours later, exhilarated, exhausted, and hungry, I was at the pavilion with my parents. There was also a couple with a baby in a carriage. The baby looked like a new one and it was sleeping while the dad rolled the carriage back and forth. I wondered if they had older children running around the park like Sean and I did. The couple looked like they were talking about something serious. I wished I could talk to that baby and ask it what it remembered about being in Heaven with God before it got born. I think we forget stuff as we get more into the world. I sure couldn't remember what it had been like.

Another half hour passed, and Sean did not show up. I saw that our parents began to worry.

"Where could he be?" asked Mom.

"I have no idea. We're going to have to look for him. Call Ozzie. He might bark," Dad said.

They instructed me to stay put while they looked for Sean and Ozzie. While I leaned against wooden fencing, gazing out over the crowds, in my mind I saw Ozzie standing by Sean in the middle of a crowd. I heard the dog speak to me, telling me where they were.

We are still near the Star Flyer. You know where that is. By a cotton candy booth. Sean got turned around and forgot which way to go with all the lights and noise, Ozzie said in my mind.

I knew where to go, but there was no one to tell and I was ordered to not leave the pavilion. I didn't have my phone with me because I was afraid it would fall out of my pocket when I was turned upside down on a ride. Besides, no one would believe me. For once, I did what I was told.

After about another half hour, I saw my parents and Sean

CHAPTER TWENTY-TWO

NOW THAT SCHOOL WAS OUT, I looked forward to my grandmother, Ellen, coming across the mountains to pick up us boys and Ozzie. We were going to stay a couple of months with her. I couldn't wait to ride her horses, and go camping and fishing with my cousin, Dillon, who lived near her. Dillon was fourteen, older than me and Sean, but we all got along.

I thought it would be fun if we could meet Grandma halfway at a place called Hanging Lake. It was a 1.5 mile climb to the top of a mountain where the lake was suspended in a crater formed by an ancient volcano. I had heard about the lake from Brian. His parents took him and his little brother there one summer. I knew stuff about it because I looked it up online.

"Mom, do you think we could meet Grandma at Hanging Lake this year? We could take a picnic," I asked.

"That would be fun. I haven't hiked to Hanging Lake since before you boys were born. I'll check with Dad and Grandma." I wanted to see Mom have fun.

Everyone agreed to meet, though Grandma groaned at the thought of the climb. She wasn't a kid anymore.

I was dressed in jeans, red T-shirt, and black tennis shoes when we met in the parking lot at the trailhead. Everybody with Ozzie walking into the pavilion. Mom told me they found Sean standing with the dog in the middle of a crowd, just like I saw him. I told them about what I saw in my mind, but they didn't believe me.

"You were just worried about Sean, that's all," said Mom. I felt alone, but I just asked if we could get something to eat now.

hugged. Except for Sean. He hugged Ozzie. Sean had on similar clothing, but his T-shirt was green, his favorite color. Both of us wore purple Rockies baseball caps. I was glad to see that Grandma's friend, Susan, had come along to pet-sit Ozzie. He wasn't allowed on the trail. She was prepared for several hours of wait time with an audio book to listen to. She brought other sources of entertainment, as well as a ball to play with Ozzie, food, and water.

Excited, Sean and I ran lickety-split for the rock-strewn trail and started climbing. Both of us ignored Mom's shout that we needed sunscreen. The adults, wearing jeans, special shirts designed to pull sweat away from skin, straw hats, and hiking boots, carried backpacks filled with bottles of water, food, and first aid gear.

As I climbed, I saw the adults carefully walking over small sliding rocks along the way. Sean and I raced each other to the top. Bigger and stronger, Sean reached the emerald green-colored lake first and shouted with glee.

I was astounded by the beauty of the lake. On two sides, there were giant waterfalls. I saw that Sean and I could walk behind one of them. We played a while, then raced back down the mountain to encourage our parents and Grandma. They were about halfway up now.

"Come on, Dad!" I shouted.

"We'll get there," Dad said.

"Grandma, you doin' okay?"

"Like Dad said, we'll get there," she said with a chuckle as she pushed her brown hair off her sweating face. She was long-legged like Mom, so I thought she should be able to take longer steps. Maybe when you are old, you have to be more cautious.

We chugged water from Mom's bottle, then raced back to the top again. Sean decided to explore off trail as we walked back to the adults. I immediately felt alarm.

"Sean, I don't think you should do that. You could get hurt," I told my brother.

"Nah. This is a piece of cake. You go your way and I'll go mine," Sean said.

I felt discouraged that Sean wouldn't heed my warning, but what could I do? Both of us began clambering down the slope.

After a few minutes, I heard Sean yell in pain. I ran to where I last saw him.

"Are you all right?" I yelled to Sean.

I saw that he was further down the side of the mountain than me. He looked stuck. He also looked sunburned on his face. I touched my own face—ouch. I was also burned. I was mad that Sean had not taken my advice. But then, we didn't take Mom's advice about the sunscreen either.

"No. A rock slid against me and knocked me down. Now I'm pinned," yelled Sean. "Get Dad."

I scrambled the rest of the way to the family. I was scared for Sean. I could see blood on his head.

"Dad, Mom, Grandma," I yelled. "Sean's hurt. Over this way."

I started back up the trail to the place I left Sean. I struggled to get the large rock off Sean's shoulder. I couldn't move it at first. I tried harder, afraid I was going to lose my footing.

"Does it hurt?" I asked my brother.

Sean winced and tried not to scream as I rolled the rock away. I had a sweatshirt tied around my waist and I put that over Sean. He was shivering. He had gotten soaked under the waterfall.

I pulled at Dad's hand as the adults arrived. Dad had first aid training, something he took once he realized that rowdy boys have accidents.

"Are you in pain, Sean?" Dad asked.

Sean was crying. "Yes, right here," he said, pointing to his shoulder which looked like it was out of place.

"Your shoulder looks out of place. Your collarbone might be cracked, too."

"His head is bleeding," I said, full of anxiety. I didn't need to tell him the obvious.

Dad opened his first aid kit and pulled out supplies. He used a bandage soaked in alcohol to clear the blood.

"Ouchouchouch," yelled Sean.

"I know it hurts but I have to clean the wound," said Dad.

It looked as though Sean had a small scrape on his forehead.

"All that blood," I said, shocked.

"Head wounds bleed a lot. He might have a concussion," Dad said.

I was worried. Why hadn't I seen a vision of Sean getting hurt? Sure, I had a feeling that he should be careful, but I didn't know he would get hurt. What did this mean? Did it mean my mind was broken? Was I going to see visions again? I wasn't sure, but I was thankful Sean wasn't badly injured. It could have been worse. Maybe next time he'll listen to me.

CHAPTER TWENTY-THREE

I LISTENED as Mom called for an ambulance to come from the nearby town of Glenwood Springs. It was lucky that she had a signal from on the side of the mountain like that. Hanging Lake is overhung with rock in Glenwood Canyon. When we are deep in the Canyon by the lake, we never have a signal on our phones.

"Dispatcher, my son is injured and needs to go to the hospital," she said. "We are about halfway up the Hanging Lake trail."

I could hear both sides of the conversation because they were talking loud over the noise of wind blowing the trees and rushing water.

"How old is the boy?" the dispatcher asked.

"Twelve."

"Let me connect you to the ER doctor. She can tell you what to do while you wait for the ambulance. "Can you stabilize him and get him down the mountain?"

"Yes, I think so. My husband has a first aid kit."

"I have one on the way. They will meet you in the parking lot. Here's the doc."

"Thank you. Doctor?"

I heard someone say, "Yes, I'm Dr. Anaheim. Is your boy conscious?"

"Yes. He looks as though his right shoulder is displaced. My husband said he might have a cracked collarbone, and he has a scrape on his forehead. He might have a concussion. A rock slid into him and pinned him. We have a first aid kit."

"Give him ibuprofen for the pain if you have it. I wouldn't give him aspirin, though. It might make the bleeding worse. Make him drink water. Can you make a sling to hold his arm to his body?"

"Yes. My husband is doing that."

"That's all you can do right now. Help is on the way. We are expecting you."

"Thank you, Dr. Anaheim."

I watched as she made Sean drink water and take Advil. I beamed love to Sean with my eyes while Dad made a splint holding the arm to Sean's body. He used the sweater and a piece of fallen wood. With the shoulder stabilized, Dad cradled and lifted my brother and began to gingerly descend the mountain. The women helped keep Sean from moving.

I said to their backs, "I told Sean not to go in that direction. I felt like he would get hurt."

Everyone was so focused on being careful with Sean who was crying in pain, they didn't even hear me. I was talking to the wind. They wouldn't have believed me anyway. I was alone. And just a little ticked off. Sean was getting all the attention. Again.

I saw the ambulance arrive about the same time as the family. They were flashing lights but not sounding the siren by the time they arrived. I was glad because siren sounds hurt Ozzie's ears. Susan and Ozzie greeted everyone. The attendants jumped out and brought a gurney with them as they headed our way. They loaded Sean on the rolling bed, careful not to bump his head or shoulder. One guy put a blanket over him.

"How does a blanket help him?" I asked Dad. The day was so hot.

"It will keep him warm so he doesn't go into shock. When you get hurt like he is, your body's energy goes straight to the injured places so you might get cold. If that happens, shock happens," he explained.

I felt scared for Sean. I was sure he felt the same way. He was making a whimpering sound. I saw tears on his face. Poor Sean. I hoped he wasn't hurting too much.

I watched as Mom got into the ambulance with Sean. The rest of us got in the family car and followed the ambulance a few miles to the ER.

It turned out that Sean did not have a concussion or cracked collarbone, just a dislocated shoulder. While the doctor and a nurse treated Sean, I asked what would happen now.

"Will we go on with Grandma, or do we have to go back home?" I asked.

I saw Mom and Dad and Grandma look at each other.

Mom spoke up, "I think we should take you both back home. Let Sean rest for a week or so."

"I agree," said Dad. He'll be quiet at home. At Grandma's there's a lot of excitement. We'll bring both of you back over as soon as Sean feels well."

"I think that's a good idea," said Grandma.

"Well, I guess," I said, disappointed.

I sat in front with Dad so that Mom could sit in the back with Sean stretched across the seat, his head in her lap. She was stroking him, keeping him quiet. For once, Sean did not resist being touched. I saw that Ozzie stayed on the floor in the rear, his head resting on the edge of the seat where Sean was lying. Grandma and Susan went back to her house.

"Call as soon as you get home. I want to know how Sean is doing," she said to Mom.

"I will," Mom replied.

I felt like Sean was in good hands, but I was also jealous. I told Sean not to go off the path and he didn't listen to me. Sean always gets attention. Now instead of spending time with Grandma having fun, I have to go home with my parents and Sean. Hopefully he heals soon so we can go to Grandma's house.

CHAPTER TWENTY-FOUR

BY THE FOLLOWING WEEKEND, Sean was his old self, so our parents drove us to Grandma's home. I knew we would have a lot of adventures at her ranch. I thought we would spend much of our time with her two horses, Lady and Jaguar. One had belonged to our dead grandpa, Bill. As soon as we arrived at the ranch, Sean and I raced each other to the barn, Ozzie at Sean's heels. So was Grandma Ellie's dog, Jetta, and her black cat, Pepper, who followed us everywhere.

Sean especially related to the horses. Grandma often had to order him into the house for meals, baths, and bed. She didn't have to order me. I always wanted to please her because she didn't believe my gift. I wanted to win her over so I gave her no trouble, hoping she would come to understand me more and that one day she would believe me when I told her about my dreams and visions.

On a clear May morning, Grandma had just completed feeding her horses and was returning from the barn when we and the dogs, and Pepper, came out of her house.

"We're taking Jetta and Ozzie for a walk," said Sean.

"Okay. See you in a bit. Don't go up the mountain."

Heedless of her instruction, we raced each other up a deer

trail. Near the top of the mountain, we found snow on the ground, even though it was May. We began kicking the snow that covered the higher grasses onto each other as we ran through the woods.

"Grandma said for us to not go this high," I said.

"I know. But do you see any danger? I want to play in the snow," replied Sean.

"There isn't any left on the ground at the ranch," I said.

"That's because the ranch is a thousand feet lower in elevation. We had a segment on weather in my science class. For every 500 feet above sea level, you can expect a change in the weather in this area," said Sean.

We stopped in a meadow and began to throw snowballs at each other. Jetta acted as if this was a game she could also play. Ozzie, a water dog, was always up for anything wet. Jetta began trying to catch the snowballs as they flew between us, grabbing the packed snow in her mouth where it melted. She shook her head to get that wetness out of her mouth and off her face. Jetta loved snow but hated getting wet. We cracked up with laughter at her antics. We began to fall backwards in the snow, making angels by waving our arms in broom-like sweeps. Then we jumped up and started running again.

As we nearly topped the hill, a sharp "crack" sound split the sky. The scent of warm musky blood assaulted the breeze. There was a clatter of hooves and we, the dogs and cat jumped off the path as deer rushed by.

We were terrified and we all took off, running as fast as we could back down the mountain to Grandma Ellie's house. We were afraid a hunter was near. Neither of us knew much about guns but we went hunting with Grandpa one year. That crack was the sound of a rifle, I was sure.

We and the dogs and cat dashed into the adobe house with its red-tiled roof, stumbling into the mudroom. I arrived first so Sean slammed the back door. We shook moisture off ourselves as we ran through the house, shouting "Grandma! Grandma!"

She jumped up when she heard us and halted us in the kitchen before we reached her brown-carpeted office where she had been working.

"Boys, what's wrong?" she asked, shock in her voice, as she ran to greet us.

"Get back in the mudroom with those wet shoes," she admonished as she almost slipped in a puddle on the Saltillo tile-covered floor. We ran back to the mudroom and tore off our wet tennis shoes.

I was the first to catch my breath but still I was spluttering when I said, "We were just playing with Jetta and Ozzie in the snow. Then there was this sharp sound! I knew it was a rifle. I knew there was a hunter near. The deer came running toward us, a bunch of them, does, I think. I didn't see any antlers."

Sean added between gasps for air, "We got out of the way fast. The deer were so scared, I don't think they even saw us."

"I could smell the blood. The hunter killed one, I'm sure," I said. I felt my eyes bugging wide with fear.

"I told you to not go up the mountain. You were in danger. Don't go there again. I know you had fun, but that was too close to hunting territory, both man and four-legged predators. This is not hunting season, but poachers could be out there. We'll walk together and I will show you where you can go on my land," Grandma exclaimed.

While we caught our breaths, she asked, "Would you boys like some hot chocolate?"

Knowing the answer without being told, she moved to the pantry and got out the dark cocoa, marshmallows, and sugar, placing them on the counter. She poured milk into a pan and began heating it over the gas flame of the stove.

"Why do people kill deer?" I asked, no longer gasping. "They are so beautiful and they don't hurt anybody."

Both of us were settled around the kitchen table, the dogs wrapped around our bare feet. The table and chairs were hand-carved by Grandpa and made of pine.

She said, "There was a time not so long ago when deer were killed for food by the people who lived here before settlers, the Native Americans, and then for the same reason by newcomers to America. They didn't have big grocery stores where they could go to buy food like we do now. They had to farm and hunt for food. You've studied American History, haven't you?"

"Yeah, but ... *now* why do they do it?" I questioned.

"I guess it's just that hunters like the challenge of tracking and killing animals. It's like a game for them. And as for the deer, well, my father told me a story when I was little about how the deer are giveaway animals."

"What does that mean?" asked Sean, sipping his yummy hot cocoa with a melting marshmallow on top.

"Well, it's sort of like deer know part of their purpose is to be food. Every living creature has a purpose. They know they are prey. They give their lives so other animals have food."

"I saw that once on TV," I said. "On that old show *Little House on the Prairie* that you watch sometimes, Grandma. The family was starving because a storm had destroyed their crops. The dad went hunting for food. He didn't want to kill an animal, but his family was starving. He saw a deer and the deer just stopped and looked at Pa. It was like an understanding between them, then Pa shot it. Then he told the deer he was sorry for taking its life and said a prayer of thanks to it."

"Yes, that's how it should be, always. Even when you pick vegetables out of the garden, you should say 'thanks' because those plants give their lives so you can have food. And if you see an animal that's been killed by a car or for whatever reason, be sure to say a little prayer. Every time you pray or send a blessing to another, it's the same as calling angels to Earth to help," she said. "Angels can help when they are asked."

"I saw blood on one of the does, on her side, like a big slash," I said, still feeling hyper.

"Maybe she got hurt earlier. Could be that a cougar chased them before the hunter spotted them. Could be they ran from the cougar right into the sight of the hunter," Grandma speculated.

"You have cougars near your house?" I asked, incredulous.

"Yes, but not close. You guys went much too far from home with your walk. I warned you to not climb the mountain. Coyotes are up there, too. Anywhere there are prey animals, like deer, there will also be predators like cougars and coyotes. It's the way of nature," she explained.

CHAPTER TWENTY-FIVE

LATER, Sean and I, wearing dry blue jeans and long-sleeve, striped polo shirts, and socks, sat around the table again, having a lunch of grilled cheese sandwiches and homemade tomato vegetable soup.

As we finished lunch, our cousin, Dillon, age fourteen, came over. He had dark brown hair and brown eyes like his mom, Chris. He was dressed in jeans and a hoodie with a logo of a bear, the mascot of his school, on it. I told him the story of our morning encounter with a hunter, with Sean filling in small details. Dillon loved to hunt deer and ducks with his uncle Tony every year. He began to tell us what that was like.

I was spellbound as Dillon told about shooting his first deer the previous winter. I was also mortified. Dillon still had the skull and antlers in his room, he told us.

I paid rapt attention as Dillon told us, "If we are hunting deer, we get up super early to hunt. It's still dark. We're set up and ready to shoot before the sun comes up. We have lots of friends who have leases so we hunt in different places.

"We get up in a blind, like a tree house, so we can see them coming. We put out some corn for them so they will come our way. For deer, I use a Remington 770 with 30-06 bullets. That gun will kick real hard. The deer I shot was walking toward me."

As soon as Dillon said those words, I popped into a vision of a deer walking toward me. In the vision, I was the one with the gun. The scene was so real, I could smell pine trees. From the blind in an oak tree, it seemed I could see the whole forest. I saw that the deer sensed I was there because the animal turned, walking away from me. I shot. I saw a bullet hit the deer in the back and go through to his chest. I saw the deer fall, dead right then.

Dillon was still talking. "It might take an hour, or even all day for them to show up. But that's the best part, really. Going out with friends and family that matter to you, being in nature, so peaceful, watching different animals," Dillon related.

"I just saw in my mind the whole thing as it happened to Dillon. The deer died immediately. He had turned around to walk away from you," I said.

"That's just how it happened," said Dillon.

I saw that he was wondering how I knew about that. He stared at me for a heartbeat, and then continued his story.

"It's kinda spooky, walking through woods in the dark, staying quiet as possible. But it's exciting," said Dillon. "That stag I shot gave us food for a year. We always eat what we kill."

Though Dillon was a bit older than us, we enjoyed playing video games together. We went into the game room.

"I like a game that involves role-playing as a policeman who catches bad guys," I said.

"What is that game like?" asked Dillon.

"You go to the website and make your own game. You can join groups," I explained.

"All that is interesting to you?" Dillon asked.

"Yes. I want to be a police officer," I said.

I continued by telling a story of one game I had played.

"I had one situation in which another officer made a traffic stop. I decided to follow the offender as he pulled away after getting a ticket. Soon, he stopped on the edge of a cliff. He was going to jump but I stopped him and put handcuffs on him. I drove him to a mental hospital where he stayed overnight. The next morning, I went to see him and gave him a ride home. The point of the game is to role-play like in real life. Be as real as possible. Act like you are not in the game. You can be whatever you want."

I listened when Sean chimed in, "I like to play a game where you build things out of different materials. I like to create many things at the same time. The possibilities are endless."

Sean had the mind of an engineer.

We all liked to play a race car game, so we went with that. "Which car do you want?" Sean asked Dillon.

"I like the GTO. Grandpa Bill had one of those, a green one."

"Noah, what do you want to play with?"

"I'm going to go with the purple Challenger."

"Noah! You always pick the Challenger. You know I like that one best," shouted Sean, waving his arms and twisting his body.

I saw Ozzie attempt to herd Sean away to a quiet place where he could calm down from his outburst of temper.

I know Sean has trouble socializing—a symptom of autism. Sometimes, he says, he feels all buzzy. He usually recognized this feeling as an oncoming outburst. He would go someplace quiet, like into his large closet. He knew when he needed a few minutes of no stimulation. But that didn't happen this time.

I was familiar with these outbursts. I made eye contact with Sean and filled him with love. Grandma didn't know about my technique, though, and escorted Sean to his room, not as punishment but giving him space where he could find quiet, just like when we were home.

Dillon and I continued with the race car game. "I'll take the black Barracuda. Grr-rr-r-rr," I said. After a while, Sean came back to the table, looking subdued, but did not join the game.

As we played, making lots of growling and crashing sounds,

we yelled encouragement to our respective cars as if the cars could hear us. I saw that Grandma was working in her office again, but she was also somewhat paying attention to our talk.

I was in awe of Dillon because this year, he had become old enough to drive a full-sized car at the local racetrack. Dillon helped his dad build a car for him to drive.

I knew that Dillon's dad, Preston, was a gearhead. Stock car driving was his passion and he had raced at the track for many years. I had heard the story that when Dillon was only four, Preston bought a little blue go-cart for him and began teaching him to drive. This season, I heard, Dillon won Rookie of the Year driving his own stock car.

I was interested in Dillon's racing experiences. Dad had given a few driving lessons to Sean, who would be old enough in a few years to get his learner's permit, but that was a long way from the excitement of a racetrack. I was still too short to see over the steering wheel. I couldn't yet reach the pedals on the floor, either.

"What kind of car do you drive?" I asked. I like talking about cars.

"It's an Oldsmobile Cutlass body with a 355 Chevy alcohol-powered engine. These cars don't use regular gasoline. You have to have a certain style to the body for this class of racing," Dillon explained.

A loud crash sound between the cars we were playing with brought Grandma back to our conversation. I saw her look at us.

"We work on my car about every day after school. Racing season starts next week and me and Dad want the car to be ready."

I know Grandma wasn't crazy about this dangerous sport. She talked with me about it during an earlier visit. But she had learned to live with it over the years since Dillon's dad got interested. I think she was glad Dillon and Preston were involved together in an activity they both loved.

"Could we go to one of Dillon's races this summer?" I asked her.

"Sure. I don't see why not. I'll make a plan with Preston."

CHAPTER TWENTY-SIX

AT BEDTIME, I was still wondering about the deer. As I drifted into deep sleep, I dreamed about the injured doe. I asked her where she lived. I wondered about her injury. She told me the hunter's bullet just grazed her flank. She asked me if I would like to walk with her. Through the night, the doe and her deer family and me, in my dream, traveled down a mountain and through the woods near Grandma's house, across another meadow and through a park, pawing the snow-covered grass for food all along the way. We went on to a cherry orchard where the deer munched on dried cherries still clinging to lower branches. There was dried brown grass under our feet. Down across another road, we visited an apple orchard where the deer also plucked leftover fruit off lower branches of the trees. Still in motion, we followed a trail through another wooded area, then circled back to the park. There, alongside a stream, I could see where the herd bedded down for the night. Tall grasses were all crushed from their bodies.

The next morning, I told Grandma of my dream while she made pancakes and bacon for us. Both of us have hearty appetites.

"Can we take a hike after we clean stalls this morning?" I

asked. "I think we would be able to track the migration path of the deer."

"Well, there aren't any deer this low during summer. They get chased down to this level when hunting season starts in September. And they really come down when snow covers the grasses they eat. We get snow, too, but not as heavy. They can paw through snow for food here."

"When I look up the hill, though, I can see permanent trails," I said.

"True. We can take a look. The trails you see are going uphill, though. The orchards in your dream run along the lower area of the ranch."

After chores, the three of us and the dogs walked out. The air was nippy this morning so along with jeans and long-sleeve shirts, Grandma and us boys wore blue windbreakers. Pepper started with us, but I saw him get distracted by some small creature in the tall grass. We found a permanent deer trail that cut across the ranch and into a cherry orchard. It was easy to see the trail, though the deer were not around. From last winter, there were still a few piles of small, dark brown pellets of deer poop along the way.

"Look, Grandma," I said. "You can see where they have pulled dried cherries from the lower branches, even though the branches are starting to turn green with leaves."

"There are still some on the ground," said Sean. "I hope they can find enough food every year to get them through winter."

I picked a cherry off the ground and threw it at Sean's head, but missed. Sean glared at me. I shrugged and gave him my best smile. I couldn't resist.

"Animals have instincts that help them find food, even if it is covered with snow. They have other migration routes, too," Grandma said.

We came to a narrow farm road and crossed it to the next orchard, one where apple trees grew. We could see the deer trail circled the budding trees. As we followed those to the far edge of the field, the path turned back toward the cherry orchard.

At last, we came to a park that had a stream running along one edge. The tall grass was crushed along the bank, looking as though the deer slept there. Sean, not realizing the water was flowing up underneath some of the tall grass, got too close to the edge and fell in. Ozzie jumped in after him, grabbing his jacket to keep him afloat.

Sean was screaming and thrashing so much that Grandma, following Ozzie into the water, could not catch him to pull him out. I looked on in horror but made myself be quiet so I could make eye contact with Sean and send him love. That was hard to do with all the racket of the dogs, Sean, and Grandma. I knew that if I could do that, Sean would settle down enough for Grandma to pull him out. I locked eyes with Sean. He was off to one side of Grandma, though, and she did not see how I helped. She and Ozzie got freezing Sean out of the water. Teeth chattering, we all ran for the warm house and dry clothes. I felt alone.

After eating some hot soup, I texted Mom and Dad about what happened on the walk. They made an anxious phone call to Grandma. She assured them Sean was okay and talked to them about taking the boys to see Dillon race.

———

That weekend, Sean, Ozzie, Grandma and I went to the racetrack to watch Dillon drive. Jetta stayed home with Pepper. Jetta didn't usually act like it, but I knew the dog was old. Sean and Ozzie and I got to accompany Dillon and his dad to the pit where crews were busy tuning, adjusting, and tweaking the cars in every imaginable way. We all did well to stay out of traffic.

Dillon said to us, "Every time we go out, we get a lot better information about what tuning needs to happen. The best part is that everyone goes all out to win. You have a team with you, and they are all supportive. But mostly it is just me and my dad in this together."

I could not believe the roaring noise during the races. I asked Dillon, "Can you wear earplugs? The noise is awful. You'll get long term hearing loss, both you and your dad."

"No. I have to hear every little thing that is happening to the car so I can adjust," answered Dillon.

I was overwhelmed by smells. I said to Grandma, "Do you smell overheated tires?"

"That's to be expected," she said.

I could also smell pungent odors of beer and food. As I walked past the bathrooms, I thought I'd throw up from the smell of urine and poop. I felt blinded when I looked up at the lights stationed around the track and parking lot. But all that left my mind when the action began.

The family sat near the top of the stands, except for me. I wanted to be close to the track. As I climbed down the bleachers, a thought sparked in my mind. I saw myself sitting in the fourth row. In an instant, a car crashed into the wall and a tire bounced over the fence, landing smack where I planned to sit. I changed my mind and went back to the top with Sean and Grandma and Ozzie.

A few minutes later, that very crash happened. The tire would have hit me with high velocity. I likely would have been killed.

"Grandma," I yelled. "I saw that wreck happen in my mind and decided not to sit there."

"You were feeling the drama," she said. "You will be able to calm down when we get home."

I felt alone, but for once, I saved my own life by paying attention to my thoughts. The race was delayed for a few minutes while the wrecked car was pulled from the track. The driver wasn't hurt.

Later in the events, Dillon was doing well but something went wrong with his engine. I watched as he pulled into the pit.

He didn't return to the track. We went down to the pit and said goodbye to him.

"Better luck next time," I said.

"Yeah. Me and Dad will be busy fixing the car all week. There's always tiny tweaks to make it run better," he said.

CHAPTER TWENTY-SEVEN

THE NEXT MORNING, I went to the barn to help Grandma feed and care for the horses. I had been looking for a quiet time when I could ask her about seeing Mom looking sad sometimes.

I pulled a barn apron over my clothes. It was kind of long for me, but I folded it at the waist and tied it back.

While I watered the horses, I asked, "Grandma, I know Mom is happy being married to Dad, and I know she loves being our mom, but sometimes I see her looking at some place far away and she looks sad. Have you noticed?"

Before she could respond, Sean walked into the barn.

"Sean, have you ever noticed how Mom gets a faraway sad look in her eyes?" I asked.

"I've seen her do that a couple of times," he said.

While Grandma forked alfalfa hay into the feeding troughs for the horses, she talked to us about what was happening at home.

"I want you to understand that nothing that goes on with your mom or between your parents has anything to do with you. They love both of you. They love each other, too."

"Well, sometimes I do feel like maybe I did something wrong that caused them to be so mad," said Sean in a sad voice.

I was done with watering, so I rolled up the hose and grabbed a bridle and began applying saddle soap to it to keep it soft.

"They fight about money, so I feel like I should not ask for things I need sometimes," I added.

"Never feel like you can't ask for what you need, Noah. They fight about money but that is just like a symptom of what is really going on," she said.

"So, what *is* going on?" asked Sean. "I do know they love each other and they love us. Why does Mom look unhappy sometimes?"

Finished feeding, Grandma took Lady out of her stall and began brushing her. Sean got a rake and started cleaning out the stall, gathering the poop into a pile, then shoveling it into a wheelbarrow.

"They do have love between them. Love is the only thing that is real. We come into this life through the essence of love. But when two people love each other and get married, after about five years, one or both naturally start to change. Each of us has our own path to follow in life. There are glorious years while the paths of married people are the same, but eventually, the paths of one or both might diverge. They could become separated in their interests, maybe, or values.

"You know I was married to a man named Jim before I met your grandpa. We loved each other, but while Jim stayed the same, after a few years, I began to grow and change. We had three children, as you know, and I stayed with the marriage for eleven years because of them but eventually, I had to get away. I felt like I was smothering. We went to counseling. He pleaded to stay together, not understanding what had happened to our love. I know this is hard to grasp because I am talking about feelings and thoughts, but when you think back, you'll get it.

"In front of the counselor, he said to me, 'I haven't changed.'"

"My heart ached for him and for our children, but I said, 'I know. But *I* have changed. This is not your fault.' There is no fault. Just natural progression in a different direction."

"How sad, Grandma," said Sean.

"It was. It still is. But I had to go. I don't know if this will happen to your parents. But if it does, just know that change and growth are natural, and it doesn't mean they don't still love each other or you."

"I get it," I said.

But I still felt sad. I hoped this didn't happen in our family.

The bridle was looking good, so I started putting oats in separate feed buckets in the stalls.

"Remember last summer when you stayed with me? You both attended an Earthbeat Music Camp. The director, Karen D'Atillo, had been a friend of the musician John Denver. Though he died years ago, there are many in this area where he lived who keep his music alive, including Karen. She taught you some of his songs."

"I love that music," said Sean, as he continued to rake.

"Do you remember a famous song called 'Rocky Mountain High?'"

"Sure," I said.

"There is a line in that song that goes, 'He was born in the summer of his twenty-seventh year, coming home to a place he'd never been before.'"

"Yeah. I love that song," I commented.

"Well, that's how it often is when people reach about that age. They start becoming more of their grown-up self. There's not a thing to be done for it. They simply grow and change, and their life has to change with them."

"So maybe that is what has happened to Mom?" asked Sean.

His eyes were filled with comprehension.

"It could be."

I was sad thinking about what could happen to our family. I didn't want my parents to fall apart. I wanted our family to be together, always. I wondered if I could see a vision of what would happen in the future. If I could, I'd try to warn my parents so they wouldn't fall apart. I didn't want to think about it anymore, so I thought about the song and the time we spent at camp. "That was fun. I'd like to go to the music camp again this year. Could we?"

"Sure. It starts on Monday."

"Oh, good. I think I would like to learn to play guitar. Maybe I could get one for Christmas."

I saw Grandma smile.

I thought if I dropped a hint about a guitar, Grandma would catch on. My plan worked.

We worked inside the barn quietly after all that, each with our own thoughts. There was a lot to think about. When we came to a stopping place, Sean took the wheelbarrow to the dung pile and emptied it. Grandma took off her barn shoes and apron. Then we went inside for breakfast. Grandma washed her hands and face and started making pancakes.

"You boys clean up."

CHAPTER TWENTY-EIGHT

SOON IT WAS time to go to music camp. We were so happy to see Karen and the other musicians who helped her, as well as the twenty other kids who came. We sang several songs, having a hoot with "Grandma's Feather Bed." We got carried away making oink, oink sounds for the piggy and cluck, clucks for chickens, and quack, quack for ducks, laughing so hard we could barely sing.

I had noticed at home that Sean was just old enough for his voice to start to change. Every now and then, he would be speaking and his voice would crack to a different octave. We were singing a John Denver song called "The Hawk and the Eagle." When we got to the part where the eagle is flying high-hi-gh-hiiiigh, Sean's voice cracked. All of the kids and three instructors started laughing, including me. Then I saw the stricken look on Sean's face as he bolted from the music room, out the back door and into some woods. Karen could not leave the other kids to follow so she nodded to me to go after him.

"Sean! Sean!" I shouted, crashing through thick brush and trees.

I could not hear a response, so I stopped and got quiet. I

thought if I did that, I would hear Sean running but after a couple of minutes, I still could hear nothing.

In my mind, I saw Ozzie running back toward me.

Come with me. Let's go, Ozzie said.

I followed the image of the dog to where Sean had fallen.

"Sean, are you okay?"

"My wrist hurts."

"Let me see."

"Ouch!"

"Can you walk?"

"Help me up. Here, pull on the other arm."

Sean and I and Ozzie walked back to the music room. Sean was crying with pain a little as walking over rough terrain jostled his wrist.

When we arrived, Karen told the other kids to take a break. Her helpers took over and got the group started on an art project. She looked at Sean's wrist and thought it was sprained.

She called Grandma, who took us and Ozzie to the urgent care center nearby.

I saw a woman with a stern look about her come toward us. Her name tag said "Liz Lincoln, P.A."

"What does P.A. mean?" I asked Grandma while the woman looked at Sean's wrist.

"It means she's a nurse practitioner. She can do anything a doctor can do except prescribe medicine," responded Grandma.

The P.A. agreed the wrist was sprained. She wrapped it and Sean was given Advil for pain. He was given instructions to stay quiet for a couple of days. I told Grandma how Ozzie spoke to me, telling me to follow. She didn't believe me, though. I felt alone.

The next morning, I went out to help feed the horses while Sean nursed his wrist. Grandma still had the gorgeous red roan Jaguar that had been Grandpa's. She also had an Appaloosa she called Lady. This horse was smaller than the roan. She was white with a black mane and tail and black spots across her rump.

As they worked, I asked, "Grandma, do you think I could have a horse of my own?"

"Wow. Where did that idea come from?"

"I've been thinking about it for a long time. I have dreams about me and a horse racing in the wind. Doing important things too. I don't remember the details, but it is a big deal for me to be with a horse. What is important about horses?"

"In Native American lore, the Horse represents Power. Horse enables the shaman to fly and reach heaven. Humans made a great leap forward when Horse became domesticated. It's akin to the discovery of fire. Before that, humans were Earthbound. Horses were honored. They were highly-prized partners with humans."

"Is a shaman the same as a medicine man?'

"Yes. A shaman is wise and can shift between worlds. I'll tell you a story I read in the Medicine Cards.

"Dream Walker, a medicine man, was walking across the plains to visit the Arapaho Nation. He carried with him his pipe. The feather tied into his long black hair pointed to the ground, marking him as a man of peace. Over the rise of a hill, Dream Walker saw a herd of wild mustangs running toward him.

"Black Stallion approached him and asked if he was seeking an answer on his journey. Black Stallion said, 'I'm from the Void where Answer lives. Ride on my back and know the power of entering the Darkness and finding the Light.' Dream Walker thanked Black Stallion and agreed to visit him when his medicine was needed in the Dreamtime."

"I know about dreams."

"Yes, you do."

"Do different colored horses have different wisdoms?"

"In mythology, they do. A yellow horse will take its rider to the East where illumination lives. A rider of a yellow, or golden, horse can share answers he finds there to teach others.

"A red horse offers the balance of work and play. He will remind his rider to offer his teachings with humor.

"A white horse brings wisdom in power. It will carry messages for all the other horses. He will carry a rider with intention to heal those in need, to share the sacred pipe and to heal Mother Earth."

"So, Jaguar, your red horse, offers humor combined with his work."

"Yes. You've noticed how he frisks around when what you think you need is for him to settle down and get you from one place to another. He's kind of hard to ride because of his playful ways, but he and Grandpa Bill had an understanding."

"What about Lady? What's her power?"

"She's not pure white because of her breeding, but she represents the white horse. Her medicine suits me."

"I think I would like a golden horse."

"You're right. Your own medicine is similar. You find answers in your dreams and share what you learn with others."

"If I get a horse, Sean will want one too. I think he might like a black horse. He comes up with designs for to how to make things. He brings solutions out of darkness and pulls them to light."

"I think you're right. You need to talk to your parents about this. If the two of you get horses, they can stay here with Jaguar and Lady. They would be too much for me to take care of when you are home and in school, but I've been thinking of hiring some help. I'm getting too old to take good care of the two that I have. But you still need your parents' permission."

I got on the phone and told Mom and Dad about my desire to have my own horse.

"Would you like a horse, too, Sean?" I asked my brother. "Grandma said they can stay at her house."

"Yeah. Can we?" Sean asked our parents in a three-way conversation. Mom and Dad know how important interaction with animals is to Sean. He has trouble getting along with people, but animals are his friends. They agreed to the idea.

CHAPTER TWENTY-NINE

ONCE MUSIC CAMP WAS COMPLETED, Grandma, Sean and I, and the dogs trekked to a nearby horse rescue ranch. The owner, Glenda, a short muscular woman with short graying hair pulled back behind her ears, greeted us. She looked tough, like I think a horse wrangler should look. But she also seemed warm and caring around the horses.

"I get wild horses that are captured by the government. The federal government has roundups when it looks like there are too many mustangs to be supported by the land. I also accept horses from families who can't support the animals anymore. Horses have a lot of expensive needs. I get horses that have been abandoned or otherwise abused. Those require a lot of rehabilitation. They must learn to trust humans again. This takes patience and a lot of time," Glenda explained.

"Can we look at your stock? I have two horses already, but both these boys want their own. I think they are old enough," said Ellie.

"Sure. Let's walk over to the pasture. There are thirty horses there. In warm weather, they stay out of the barn most of the time."

I was stunned by the sight of all those horses of every color.

"Look Grandma. There's a golden one!" I exclaimed.

"That's a Palomino. That one was left here by owners who could not take her with them when the father's job required a move to New York. They were heartbroken to leave her. She's gentle," Glenda said.

"That's the one for me," I said.

"Do you see one that you like, Sean?" asked Grandma. Sean picked a black male horse. Glenda told him this horse had been abused and suggested he pick another one.

"No. I already understand him, and he understands me. I can tell by his eyes."

He walked up to the horse and held out his hand so the animal could get his scent.

"Be careful," cautioned Grandma.

She had no need to worry. The black horse rubbed its muzzle on Sean's hand.

While Grandma took care of the details of purchasing the horses and getting them loaded in her trailer, we got acquainted with our new four-legged friends. Glenda added a couple big bundles of hay and other supplies.

We drove home, pulling the loaded horse trailer. Grandma was careful not to make a sudden stop or otherwise jerk the trailer around. At her barn, we unloaded the horses. At first, the black horse did not want to come out. My horse walked right out onto the ground, but Sean's horse didn't like what he saw when he looked out at the step down to the ground. Grandma had some sweet oats in the barn, so Sean offered him handfuls, gradually easing him forward for more, till he made the step.

The rest of the day, Sean and I brushed, fed, and played with all the horses while Grandma made Mexican food for dinner— enchiladas, rice, refried beans, salad, and tacos. She had to order us to come in and wash up for dinner.

At the table, she told us, "We'll have to get saddles, halters, and other gear for the new horses tomorrow. Have you thought of names for them?"

"My horse is named Chance because it was just a chance I would find her today," I said.

"I'm naming mine Truxton. I think he looks strong and brave. Grandpa told me he had a stallion named that when he was a boy," Sean said.

"Grandpa knew a lot about horses. I'll get a friend of mine who is a horse trainer to come over and measure their backs, so we get the right size saddles," she said.

After dinner and clean-up, everyone watched the movie *The Horse Whisperer*. Grandma thought we would get some ideas of how to get acquainted with a horse. I thought the mushy part was gross.

When I could get away with it, I poked Sean in the arm a few times. Sean kept slapping back at me but was interested to see what happened to the horse.

Grandma kept her thoughts about the gorgeous Robert Redford to herself. I noticed her scrutiny.

"Are you thinking about that actor, Grandma?" I asked.

"Noah, no thoughts are private with you around," said Grandma, which made everyone giggle.

After we got ready for bed, taking showers, and putting on superhero pajamas, we asked Grandma if she could tell us a story about horses.

"Well, what do you think was the most important message of the movie?"

"I guess the part of how important it is to communicate with your horse," said Sean.

"That's right. I do know a story about communicating with all animals. It goes like this: One time a Native man went outside his home to the corral to meet with some friends. One of them was riding a wild horse, a mustang like some of those we saw at the rescue farm. The wild horse threw his head hard and broke his bridle. The horse saw his chance to run free again. He bucked his rider and raced down the road.

"One man jumped on another horse and chased after the

wild mustang while other friends took care of the thrown rider. The horse loved a good chase. The adventure continued through many obstacles—fences of different types. The cowboy didn't have to jump any of those fences because the mustang broke through them, clearing the path.

"After a few near-death experiences, the mustang found a pasture and stopped. The cowboy put a halter on him and doctored his wounds by cleaning them with water and putting medicine salve on them. He walked his horse and the rowdy one back home over the same route they first traveled. He saw all the obstacles they had negotiated together. He realized they had been running on the instinct of the wild horse to get away from humans, with no time to make the right maneuvers. He realized the wild horse had tendencies to lean toward and focus on the direction he wanted to go. He could see how much communication had taken place between him and this horse, without saying a word. The wild horse had shown his need to feel safe by his actions."

"That's what you have to do with your horses. You have to develop good communication with them, and they will keep you safe," she said.

Sean, Grandma, and I spent a couple of months with the new horses. We needed to get used to them, and the horses needed to recognize us. She wanted to help us to know how to train our horses. We did that by walking them around the corral and talking to them. We used sweet oats as a reward to get them to do things like come to us, halt at a certain spot, stuff like that. I asked her to tell us more about how to relate to our horses.

"You're developing a personal, one-on-one friendship with your horse. But a horse is not a dog or cat that you can spoil by feeding them people food or letting them up on the couch. Your horse will look to you as her leader. To do that, work with your horse every day for a focused half hour. That's about as long as a horse can tolerate. That much time focused on repeating a behavior is like working three or four hours for a horse. The thing you are teaching must be repeated many times. It is important to do the same thing in the same way each training period, even small things," she told me.

I absorbed this information. Somehow, I knew it would become important to have such a relationship with the horses. Like something important was going to happen. I didn't know when this important event would come about, but I knew that my knowledge and connection to the horses was vital. One of these days I'd need to communicate in my mind with the horses, and I would be ready.

CHAPTER THIRTY

ON ANOTHER MORNING walk with the dogs, Pepper decided to come along again. He was a friendly cat. As we walked, I heard songbirds chirping all over the neighborhood. A meadowlark woke me up each day as soon as the sun began to rise.

As we boys, dogs, and cat climbed a small hill, I noticed a magpie raising a ruckus around Pepper. That magpie usually called out warnings from what I had begun to call the Lookout Tree a little further up the hill from what I called the Nest Tree, but this day he was flapping his wings at Pepper. The cat crouched in tall weeds just below the Nest Tree. The magpie began dive-bombing close to Pepper's tail. Jetta had already arrived at the top of the hill, but when she heard the tone of the magpie, she raced down and chased the bird away from Pepper, who was still crouched in the weeds. The bird flew away, protesting loudly. Jetta then walked a circle of protection around Pepper, then stopped in front of the cat. Pepper reached out with his face and kissed Jetta smack on the lips. Appreciation. I was laughing my butt off throughout these antics. Sean and Ozzie were still at the top of the hill and missed all the fun.

A few morning walks later, I saw that Pepper was crouched below grasses on the other side of the trail. He was preparing to pounce on Jetta who was pretending not to notice. They liked to play a game of "You're it," taking turns chasing each other with short bursts of speed. Pepper was just about ready to pounce when I saw a mouse amble *right* under the cat's nose. Poor dumb mouse. Poor dead mouse. So much for that game. I had fun watching the antics of the pets. I sensed what they were thinking, and they knew I understood.

I knew Pepper's habit was to go out at night at 9:00 pm, then come back in at ten. One night that summer, he went out at nine but did not come back at ten, or ever after. Sean and Grandma and I traveled all over town and put up posters with a picture of Pepper on them. We put ads in the paper and asked for an announcement on the local radio station, but weeks went by and there was no Pepper. I had a dream in which I saw Pepper inside a shed that had a window at the top. I felt Pepper had found a new home and the new family was keeping him inside.

Grandma didn't believe the dream had anything to do with reality. She told me I was just using wishful thinking to help me through my grief over the loss of Pepper. But I was determined to follow my dream. I started riding Chance from ranch to ranch, widening my search every day, looking for anyone who had a new cat in their life. I found Pepper at the home of Aaron and Maisie.

"We never saw your posters. And we don't read the paper," Aaron explained.

They were keeping Pepper in a shed in their backyard at night because he would rampage in the house while they were sleeping, trying to get out.

I went back to the ranch and told Grandma. We went to the couple's home and picked up Pepper.

"Thanks for looking after him," Grandma said to Maisie.

"Oh, we like him a lot. He has so much personality," Maisie said. "If he comes this way again, I'll know where he belongs."

I was always up for more fun. I asked if we could go fishing and have a fish fry the next day. Grandma agreed. Dillon and Preston were included. Jetta and Ozzie came, too. We drove to the Crawford Reservoir before daylight. We wanted to catch the fish early when they were just waking up and hungry. We kept mostly quiet as we picked a campsite. The water was sparkling blue, like a lake I'd seen in Denver.

As we trooped to the water, Sean had to keep Ozzie leashed so he wouldn't run into the water and stir up the fish. Preston suggested we move upstream a bit. He had a favorite spot. As I gazed over the sparkling water, I saw a big rainbow trout that spoke to me. It seemed he was offering himself for food. I was so excited, I forgot for a moment that no one would believe me if I told them. I pointed to the spot where I saw the trout.

"I saw in my mind there's a big trout right over there," I whispered to Preston.

He gave me a "you are weird" look.

"Nah. I think we should go up where the water eddies around a few rocks. Fish like to hide in the shadows there," Preston said.

We moved on to a little sandy beach Preston had chosen. Preston helped us put Power Bait on our hooks. It is goopy stuff that reminds me of Play-Doh. I stuck some on my hook. My hands smelled fishy after I handled it. Everyone began casting their lines in the area where Preston directed us. Except me. I went back to where I saw the trout and cast toward that spot. Soon, I saw the tip of my line dip further into the water. I knew that meant I had a bite. I yelled for Preston to come help me. I was excited and I stepped backward at first, but then I remembered what my grandpa taught me—to start reeling the line in. I reeled slowly. I pulled out the colorful trout.

"Good job, Noah. Now, do you want to keep your fish or release it back to its life in the water?" Preston asked.

"It's so beautiful. I would rather put it back in the water," I replied.

He helped me take the hook out of the lip of the fish and I turned it loose. I felt good about that.

Though he saw the fish, Preston still didn't believe I'd had a vision about where to find it. He called me lucky. I felt angry and alone.

Sean caught a yellow perch after that, and Dillon caught a couple of smaller fish as well. There was a grill at our campsite. Preston taught us how to clean the fish and take out the bones. He started a fire in the grill and cooked a yummy fish breakfast for us. Fresh fish right out of the lake—yum! We had fun throwing sticks in the water for Ozzie. I loved watching him splash around after them.

I tried not to think about the vision I had where I saw the fish, because I was still hurt by Preston's comment. He thought I was just lucky. But it wasn't luck. I was certain one of these days I'd be able to convince someone of my ability to see things. I just didn't know if it would happen anytime soon.

CHAPTER THIRTY-ONE

A FEW DAYS LATER, I was looking bored, so Grandma suggested a trip to a toy store. We drove to a bigger town, Grand Junction, where there was such a store. On the way, Sean fell asleep. Even at his age, he needed rest in the afternoon. Grandma and I talked about her fear that Sean might have an episode in the store where there would be lights and noise. And people.

"Don't worry, Grandma. This could happen, but I can tell when Sean is on overload. He starts looking fidgety. He told me he feels buzzy sometimes."

"What should do we do if that happens?" Ellen asked.

"I can calm Sean by making eye contact and sending love to him."

"Noah, I'm not much on that idea," she said. I felt rejected and alone.

On the way to the store, I pointed out some tail lights on an Audi driving in the other lane. They were doing interesting things. I told Sean, now awake, and Grandma that when the driver of the Audi hit his brakes, the tail lights flashed a design that looked like real eyes. They had pupils and eyelashes. When the driver let off the brake, the eyes closed and all that were glowing were the tail lights in an eyelash design. All three of us laughed as we watched those bright eyes open and close like they were winking. We entered the store on a good note.

At the toy store, I found a Lego kit with parts that I could use to build a police station. Sean was thrilled to find a kit with components he could use to take his robot beyond the construction paper model. It was expensive, but Grandma would do anything for Sean. I was aware of her willingness to always please Sean. I felt jealous and alone.

On the way home, sirens and lights began flashing as a state trooper car approached, going fast. Grandma pulled to the side of the road. I was excited, jumping up and down in my seatbelt, wondering about the situation. Another highway patrol car soon followed, along with an ambulance. As we drove by, we saw a woman being pulled out of her smashed car. I spotted another crushed car over the embankment as Grandma drove past. She didn't see it because she was busy dealing with traffic. This second car had rolled between some tall bushes.

A little bit later in the afternoon, I was in a quiet state, thinking about the victims of the accident, and I fell asleep. I saw in my dream the man who was driving the car that was lying upside down over the embankment, between bushes. I watched the spirit of the man rise from his body and he looked down at it curiously, wondering why he wasn't in it now. I saw the man was not in pain anymore. His spirit looked peaceful. I realized the man died.

"Grandma, I had a dream about another car in that accident. It was flipped over the embankment. I saw the man who had been driving that car. I saw him die."

"Gosh, Noah, I hope not. I think you were just reacting to the shock of it all."

I felt disappointed and alone. Grandma didn't get local news in the country, so we didn't see a report. I wondered, though, what happened when people die. I asked Grandma.

"Death is a natural part of life and when people or animals

die, they move on to the next step in their soul journeys. They move to a place of no conflict. They can still feel the love they have for the people left behind and they can help them feel it, too. Love is the only thing that is real."

I heard her words and wondered why sometimes I didn't feel loved. I often felt alone.

Sean and I often saddled up and rode trails around the 2,000-acre ranch. Only six acres of the land were being used for housing, pasture and garden. The rest was high desert with soaring adobe buttes and ravines. Ozzie and Jetta always went along. Dillon joined us on these rides on his grey horse, Smokey. One day, we explored a ravine with a small stream running through it. I thought this looked like a good place to plan a campout for the next night. The adults agreed but insisted on coming along. No way were they going to let us boys out in the desert alone overnight.

All of us rode up to choose a site and set up camp. I struggled to set up a couple of tents, so Preston helped me while Dillon and Sean picked up lots of dry wood for the campfire. Grandma got the fire going and put a portable grill over it. She made warm tortillas and beans for our dinner. She had chopped lettuce, tomato, and onion to add to the mix before we left home. Preston had his guitar and he played a dozen cowboy songs for us. He also had his Remington rifle. We heard coyotes howling to each other at moonrise. They seemed far away, though. Sean, Dillon, and I climbed in our sleeping bags. The adults agreed that Grandma would sleep first while Preston kept the fire going. I dreamed about coyotes approaching our fire and jumped up to tell Preston, but he didn't believe this could happen.

"Those animals are far away," he told me.

"They sound close," I argued.

"That's just because their howl echoes through the ravines. Go back to bed, Noah."

No way was I going to do that. I hid behind the boulder

Preston was leaning against. I heard Preston playing his guitar to keep himself awake. Then Preston drifted off.

A while later, I heard a noise and looked around the boulder and saw glowing eyes. I woke Preston. Hungry coyotes dared approach the camp. Preston grabbed his gun and shot toward the sky, scaring the animals away and rousing everyone. We saddled our horses as fast as we could and headed home in the dark. I think Preston began to wonder if I really did see the animals in a dream, but his gearhead mind couldn't see any logic. I was ignored again. I felt alone.

Preston and us boys went back to the campsite the next day to retrieve the gear. Animals had torn through our stuff, looking for food, I guess. I wondered if it was the coyotes.

CHAPTER THIRTY-TWO

IT WAS GETTING close to time for us to return to school. We decided to go on a trail ride and camp overnight again. Preston and Dillon joined us on their own horses. We had ridden several miles when a sudden thunderstorm burst over our heads. Rain fell in great sheets. We were looking for a cave or an overhang to get under when Truxton startled at a small creature running across his path. The holes where small creatures live underground were flooded and they were coming to the surface to keep from drowning. Truxton took off with Sean hanging on for life. Ozzie went with them. Horse, dog, and boy seemed to vanish in the pelting rain.

"Grandma, we've got to catch Truxton. Sean will be hurt!" I shouted amidst crashing thunder, lightning, and rain. All the other horses were twisting and turning with fear. Thankfully, we found a huge red rock overhang and we crowded our horses under it. I talked and petted Chance to calm her but she kept prancing and trying to get loose. Grandma's cell phone still worked, and she called other neighbors to help search for Sean. She rode with me back to her house. She was afraid I would get hurt. I was a good rider, but not an expert.

At last, we arrived at the barn. I took care of Chance.

Grandma told me to go in the house, get dry, and stay put while she went back to the search. I did not go inside as instructed. Even though I was soaked and shivering, I went to Truxton's stall and sat in a corner on the dry, fragrant hay. After a while, I fell asleep and had a dream in which Truxton came to me and showed me where to find Sean. In my mind, I saw Sean lying at the edge of a rushing stream, unconscious. I put a hackamore on Chance right quick, jumped bareback, and raced out of the barn to tell Grandma. At that moment, she arrived back at the house to look after me. I told her about my dream, but she didn't believe me.

"You were just dreaming, Noah. I know you are worried. The men will find Sean. Let's get into dry clothes. I don't want you to catch a cold," she said, reaching for Chance's hackamore.

"No," I shouted.

I turned from her grasp. The horse and I ran as fast as we could on the slippery clay trail to the stream. I found Sean unconscious right where I saw him in the dream. He was unconscious and water from the rising stream was lapping against his face. Truxton stood by with reins dangling, though he was dancing about in fear. He had come back to his boy. Ozzie was licking Sean, trying to wake him up.

Preston rode up to where I was yelling. He was an EMT. He examined Sean for injuries. He thought Sean probably had a concussion and for sure, his left arm was broken. Wiping rain from his face often, Preston pulled off his own shirt and a found piece of wood to make a splint. He placed the wood under the break on Sean's arm and wrapped the shirt around tight. Then he tied the shirt in a knot to keep the arm from moving at the break. Moving it would hurt even more.

During the search, Preston's horse had begun limping, so he dashed back to his house on foot for his powerful F-150 Raptor truck. One of the neighbors helping with the search took care of the limping horse. He took the horse back to his own ranch.

As an EMT, Preston always had a first aid kit, a backboard,

and a blanket in his truck. Grandma had called for an ambulance, but the roads were flooded, and some were washed out. I heard her tell the dispatcher to have an ambulance meet Preston's truck at the highway. Preston and Dillon loaded Sean on the board and put him in the king cab of the truck, covering him with the blanket. Dillon hopped in the truck to keep Sean stable while Preston used four-wheel drive to pick his way over the washed-out road to the highway. Grandma and I took the four other horses back to the barn, then climbed in her ranch truck to follow Preston to the hospital. We went straight to the ER to see Sean. He had regained consciousness.

"What happened?" Sean muttered.

"Truxton got scared and ran with you. He dumped you in the creek," said Preston.

"Is my horse okay?

"He's okay. He just got scared by the lightning and thunder."

A nurse pushed a portable x-ray machine to Sean's bed. I got to watch. I could see a broken place on the arm pictures.

Sean rested a few minutes while waiting for the doctor to return. A nurse brought supplies the doctor would use to make a cast. Sean cried a little more. I could tell he was scared.

"How long do I have to wear a cast?" he asked.

"Probably six weeks," the doctor said. "I'm going to put the cast most of the way down your fingers. You'll be able to move the tips of your fingers a little. You can play video games, but you can't play ball or anything like that. What color would you like on the outside of the cast?"

He showed Sean pink, blue, and green gauzes.

"I think green would be good," Sean said.

"Green it is, then," said the doctor as he finished up.

"Wow, Sean, that looks cool. Can I sign it?" I asked.

"Sure. Grandma and everyone can sign it," Sean said, a little proud, a little excited, a little scared. But medicine had dulled the pain.

I felt glad he wasn't hurting anymore. As the tension of the situation started to ease, I thought back to the moment I saw Sean lying by the stream. He was exactly where the horse told me he'd be. At some point, my family would have to acknowledge my ability to see visions. I wanted to say, *I told you so*, but I couldn't bring myself to do it. I was too happy to have my brother safe. The connection I made with both my horse and his horse had been important. Without the connection, I wouldn't have been able to find Sean.

CHAPTER THIRTY-THREE

"YOU KNOW, we are going to have to tell your parents what happened," said Grandma.

Both Sean and I groaned.

"What will we tell them?" Sean asked.

"We will tell them every detail. How Noah had a vision about where to find you. How he took off and went right to the spot where you were lying unconscious. How Ozzie and Truxton stayed with you so you were not alone. How Ozzie kept you warm by putting his body across you. How Preston got you in his truck and met an ambulance at the highway. How Noah and I followed you to the hospital. How from now on, we will believe Noah when he tells us a dream or a vision or a conversation with an animal!"

I felt nurtured. I beamed. I didn't feel alone anymore.

Our parents were shocked to hear of Sean's accident. After Grandma talked to them, it was decided they would come immediately to get us. The next day, they arrived. It was decided that we would all stay a few more nights to let Sean get better rested.

I was so happy to see them. I didn't realize how much I had missed them. Grandma cooked a big roast beef dinner for all of us. The house smelled delicious all day.

Once we were seated at the big dining table, Grandma started talking about me saving Sean's life because of a dream I had. She gave them all the details, with me and Sean interrupting with our thoughts on what happened.

"At first I was so upset with him because I told him to put on dry clothes and stay in the house while I went back to the search party and he did not do that," Grandma said.

Though I didn't want to leave Chance and Truxton, I couldn't wait to get home again. Preston was planning to load our horses during the Thanksgiving break and take them to a ranch near our house in Denver. The ranch belonged to a friend of Grandma's; a guy named Colden. He had agreed to board our horses for us during the school year.

Soon, Sean and I said goodbye to the horses and pets. I was sad to leave Chance. We would be able to ride them on weekends sometimes, though.

On the way home, I began thinking about how acting on my dream of where to find Sean in the storm had probably saved his life. It seemed to me that I could use my gift of Knowing to help others. I was thinking about Brian, about the big red C I had been seeing on his chest lately. I still felt uneasy about it. I decided to talk to Mom about it after we got home. Soon as we unpacked the car, she began doing stuff in the kitchen.

"Mom, I need to tell you about something," I said.

"What is it, Noah?"

"For a while, before school was out and we went to Grandma's, well ... whenever I would look at Brian, I would see a big red C on his chest. You know—like it was printed on his shirt, except it happened every time I saw him, no matter what shirt he was wearing."

"Noah, I promised that after your dream helped to find Sean and get him to safety, I would pay more attention to the weird things you see and hear. I believe you, now, when you tell me about this C on Brian's chest. I believe you really see it and that it is meaningful. What do you think it means?"

"I don't know, Mom. But I feel worried when I see it."

"Well, maybe we should talk to Brian's mom and dad about it. What do you think?"

"Would you, Mom? I feel I should at least tell them about my experience. They might just think I'm weird, but I should at least do that."

"Okay. I'll talk to Dad. He doesn't have to work tomorrow. Maybe we all could visit Brian's family and talk to them."

The next morning, after talking with Dad, Mom called Brian's mom, Shelley.

"Hi Shelley. It's Juliet," I heard her say.

I couldn't hear Shelley's end of the conversation, but Mom asked if we could stop over after lunch for a visit. A plan was made. I was feeling anxious all morning about what to say to Brian and his folks.

"Mom, what should I tell them?" I asked.

"We will talk to them together. We will just tell them about your gift of intuition and share with them how that intuition helped to save Sean's life."

"Then they will think I'm weird. And you, too."

"I'm willing to look weird to the neighbors, Noah. I'm willing because it is important to you to talk with them about your vision of the C on Brian's chest. Your dad and I support you in this."

I felt relief that I was no longer alone. My parents and brother *believed* me now. I felt that no matter what Brian's parents thought about me, I had to tell them about what I was seeing.

That afternoon, my parents and I walked to Brian's house. Sean didn't want to go with us. After saying hello, sitting down in the living room decorated in yellow, and catching up on our summer adventures, it was time to talk seriously to Brian and his parents.

"Shelley, I want to tell you about a serious accident that

happened while the boys were with their Grandma," my mom began.

"I can feel you have something on your mind, Juliet," Shelley said.

"I do. Let me first tell you that all his life, Noah has had dreams and visions about things that have not happened. We never took him seriously, just thought our youngest son had a vivid imagination. Even when things he 'saw' happened, we dismissed it as coincidence.

"But a couple of weeks ago, Sean was in a dangerous accident, and a dream that Noah had led rescuers to where Sean was lying unconscious at the edge of a rushing stream. Ever since that experience, Ron and I decided to start paying more attention to Noah's extra perceptions," Mom said.

"And you feel Noah has something to tell us that he has intuited about our family?" Shelley asked.

"Yes. Go ahead, Noah. Tell them what you are experiencing when you look at Brian."

My eyes felt like they were popping out. I took a deep breath. I felt scared to talk to the Jones family about this. My hands were shaking a little. I leaned forward toward Brian, who was sitting in a comfortable brown chair across from me.

"Well, I don't know what to say except, Brian, every time I've looked at you the last few months, I see a big red C printed on your chest. I don't know what it means, but I've been feeling like I should tell you and your parents about it," I said.

Brian looked at me like I was nuts. I felt so bad. His mother gasped. Both his parents looked at me like they were shocked by my words. I wanted to be anywhere except sitting in front of them. Yet, as I looked at Brian's chest, there it was, a big red C.

"I don't know what to say, Noah. I can't imagine why this is happening," Shelley said.

"Me neither," I said.

"Well. I must tell you that lately, Brian has been ill. He had symptoms of high fever and sore throat, so we took him to his pediatrician. He tested positive for strep throat. He took medicine and got well. Then, a few weeks later, the same symptoms came back. We haven't been able to get him truly well over the last two months," she said.

"Given what you are telling us now, I think we will take him back to the doctor and ask for lab work to be done," Brian's dad said.

"I'm so sorry to bring this to you. Noah has been concerned, though, and we support him," Mom said.

"I'm shocked, but we are all glad you shared your intuition with us. It's the weekend, but I'll call the doctor in the morning for an appointment," Shelley said.

After a little more chatting, my parents and I went home. We told Sean what we talked about.

"Noah, I still think you are weird. But I believe that is a good thing. You saved my life when I fell off Truxton. Maybe your weirdness will help Brian learn if he has an illness," Sean said.

I never felt so proud in my life. I felt like my family really supported me now. I was no longer alone. And that being weird was a good thing, maybe.

CHAPTER THIRTY-FOUR

SCHOOL WAS GOING to start next week, so Mom took Sean and me shopping for new clothes. We had outgrown everything we wore last school year. I always complain about shopping, but all during our trek through the stores, I was thinking about Brian. His parents were taking him to the doctor again today.

"Mom, as soon as we get home, will you call Brian's mom and ask how the doctor visit went?"

"Yes, I will. I know you are worried. I am, too."

Mom called Shelley, who invited our family to come over to their house when Dad got home from work. I felt so scared for Brian. Mom stayed busy while we waited for Dad. She made her yummy cornbread casserole for our dinner and an extra batch to take to Brian's family. As soon as Dad arrived, we all walked to Brian's house.

"Hi everyone. Come on in," Shelley said in a serious voice.

She directed us to the living room where Brian and his dad sat. Mom offered her the casserole dish which she gratefully accepted, taking it into her warm yellow kitchen, placing it on the round oak breakfast table.

I looked at Brian. Wow! I was relieved I wasn't seeing that

red C today. I kept my thoughts to myself though. Shelley started the conversation.

"Well, the doctor thought Brian's recurring symptoms could be leukemia," she said.

I gasped in horror.

"It's okay Noah. I mean, as it turns out, he does have leukemia, but it is in a beginning stage. There is a ninety-six percent chance he will recover just fine," Shelley continued.

"The doctor gave Brian some tests. He did a bone marrow aspiration through Brian's hip and a spinal tap right there in the office," Brian's dad explained.

"Did that hurt?" I asked Brian.

"It hurt a lot," Brian said, his voice trembling with tears as he remembered.

His dad put his arm around Brian's shoulder, holding him close. I felt so bad for him. A quiet moment passed between all of us.

"Brian has to be in the hospital the first week of school while the doctors test to see what kind of therapy will work best for him. Then they will know what medicine to use. Then he will likely go to the hospital every three weeks for chemotherapy infusions," Shelley said.

I was stunned. I didn't know what to say to her or Brian. Then it occurred to me that he would be missing a lot of school.

"Don't worry, Brian. I'll make sure to bring all your assignments to you when you are absent from school," I said.

He looked a little relieved, but also like he had not even thought about school yet.

———

School started. Sean now attended a middle school, but Brian and I were still at the Montessori. Now I was one of the big kids. Brian would be, too, when he could be there. I was glad I still had Mrs. Stein as my main teacher. She was the best. It seemed weird to be there without Brian, though. At the end of the week, Mrs. Stein gave me assignments to pass on to Brian.

"Tell him not to worry, though. He can do this work whenever he feels up to it. I am also sending a parent tutorial for his mom in case Brian needs help," she said.

"I can help him, too. I'll explain to him what you taught us," I said.

Brian came home from the hospital that same day. I waited till Saturday to go over to see him. When I looked at him, again the big red C was gone. I felt relieved. But Brian looked weak somehow.

"How do you feel?" I asked.

"I don't have any energy. But otherwise, I'm okay," he replied.

"What do you feel like doing?"

"We could play video games."

"Yeah. Let's do that."

We played *Car Chase* for a long time. While we played, Brian told me he would have to start treatments on Monday.

"I'm going to have to sit in a big chair with a needle in my chest. The doctor will put what they call a port in my chest, so I don't have to get an IV in my arm every time. That will make it easier. I'm scared. I'm worried about my hair falling out. I'll just have to sit there a couple of hours each time, but I can play video games. My mom will stay with me the whole time and I'll be able to come home at the end of the day. I will get a treatment every three weeks, but I'll be able to go to school most of the time," he explained.

"Oh, good. We miss you at school. Just seems like you should be there."

Every Saturday, I went to visit Brian at his house, even when he was able to attend school. After three weeks, his hair was falling out in clumps, so he decided to get his head shaved. When I got to his house, he looked strange wearing his ball cap and no hair underneath, but I tried hard not to stare. The treatments went on all year.

Summer came and Brian did not feel strong enough to play baseball. Usually after a treatment, he threw up a lot. I thought we would have a crummy season without his excellent pitching. His body handled the treatments well overall, though, and his blood count was high enough that he could come to the games and not be afraid he would pick up a virus.

I still played catcher for the team. Brian was allowed to wear his uniform but sat in the dugout and watched. After our first two losing games, the coach surprised us.

"Brian, do you feel like throwing a few pitches? I talked to your parents. They said it would be okay," Coach asked.

"Wow! I'd love to play," Brian shouted.

When he came out to the pitcher's mound, everybody in the park cheered, both teams and all the parents. We all felt he was so brave and were happy to see him feeling strong. Brian warmed up with a few throws. Then it was time to start the inning.

The first batter up was Donny of the Eagles team. The umpire watched carefully, and so did I.

"Ball one," the umpire called. I was kinda holding my breath.

The batter cued up his bat and screwed his feet around in the red dirt. The umpire dusted the home plate.

"Ball two," the umpire said.

Brian took a deep breath and squinted his eyes at me. With my fingers between my knees, I gave him a signal of where to aim the ball.

"Strike one," the umpire shouted.

Brian struck that batter out. Everybody on both teams cheered again. Even though we played against each other, all the Eagles were friends with all the Bulldogs. We all wanted to see Brian do well. He didn't play anymore that game, but the coach put him in for short periods here and there. The Bulldogs didn't lose any more games. Brian's courage made all of us more determined.

CHAPTER THIRTY-FIVE

IT WAS ALMOST time to go visit Grandma for the summer. I was looking forward to the adventures I knew we would have at her ranch. But I also didn't want to leave Brian for the summer. He was still going to be very sick with his treatments. I would miss our weekly video game sessions.

Sean usually took Ozzie for walks in the mornings before the day got hot and again in the late afternoons. We had a big back yard where Ozzie could go through his doggie door, but he liked to explore the neighborhood, too. One day, Sean was feeling crummy for some reason, so I took Ozzie out in the afternoon. I had made this trip around the block many times.

I had often noticed the house of a neighbor with many small animal cages in the backyard. The owner of the house, a woman we all called Miss Brenda, was in the yard watering her many flowers.

"Hi Miss Brenda," I called out.

"Hi Noah. Walking Ozzie today?"

"Yeah. Sean has a bellyache. Don't know why."

"Want a glass of cold tea?"

"Sure."

"Come on in the house. Bring Ozzie in. I'm done here."

As I walked through her living room into the kitchen, I saw that there were more animal cages with little critters in them like squirrels, raccoons and even mice. Also, there were plants sitting and hanging everywhere. I sat at her kitchen table, covered with a red plaid tablecloth, while she pulled a pitcher of tea out of the refrigerator and poured glasses full.

"Want some sugar in your tea?"

"No, I like it plain."

As she placed our glasses on the table, I itched to ask about the animal cages.

"You seem to take care of an awful lot of animals."

"I do. I have about a hundred right now. They come to me when they need a home or I find them injured."

"I wonder how they know how to find you."

"I don't really know. I've always taken care of injured animals. It started when I was a kid. Across from the house where I grew up, there was a cemetery. Across from the cemetery was our water tower. I lived in a small town called Milford."

"At the top of the tower, I could always see a big owl's nest. The adult owls would come there every year and raise their babies. These were big barn owls with the tufted ears. I could see the little babies with their ears. They looked like kittens to me."

"After a while, some big kids started bothering the babies. They would throw rocks and sticks at the nest. I couldn't let that happen, so I climbed the ladder on the side of the tower and picked up the two babies. I put them on my shoulders and climbed back down. The parent owls just watched me. I think they knew I was helping them."

"I took the babies home and fed them little chunks of meat. When the boys were not around, I took them back up to their nest. Again, the parent birds just watched. I repeated this process all summer until the babies flew away, if I saw the babies in danger from those boys," she said.

"The adult owls never bothered you?"

"No, they would just watch. When my dad saw me doing this, he would fuss at me. He was afraid the parent owls would attack me, or that I would fall off the ladder. That never happened. When I got out of high school and moved away, my dad took over the job, though," she said with a sweet smile.

"And now, you have about a hundred animals."

"Yes, I've always loved to rescue animals and plants. I work with rescue organizations all the time—the wildlife people and the raptor rescue people. I take care of plants too. I have at least 200 of them. I can't stand to see one that needs water or a trimming."

"I can see when an animal or plant needs help too," I said.

"I do know that about you, Noah. I see it in your energy field. You have instinctive knowing when one needs your help."

"That's true. Do animals and plants speak to you?"

"I don't really hear words, but you can tell by an animal's behavior what it is that they need. The same with plants. Noah, you can use your intuitive knowing to help them. People, too."

"Well, I did help to save my brother's life this summer."

I told her about the adventure with Sean getting lost in the storm and how I dreamed where to find him.

"You need to know that you can use your intuitive knowledge that comes through dreams or however it gets to you—you can use that to help people."

I told her about seeing the big red C on Brian's chest, and how it turned out that he had leukemia.

"The doctor says that Brian will be just fine, though. He has about another six months of treatments."

"Noah, you probably have saved Brian's life with your gift."

Soon, Ozzie and I went home. But I kept thinking about Miss Brenda and what a special person she was. And I thought that it could be that she was right.

I began to speak up when I had a dream or a vision. My family believed me. I didn't feel alone anymore.

ABOUT THE AUTHOR

Margaret Cheryl Hardy was a former journalist who loved interviewing people about their lives, holistic living, the environment, and Mother Earth. She wrote for the *Daily Sentinel* and was a featured writer for the *Augusta Times* and *Rocky Mountain News* and she also worked with non-profit organizations writing grants. Writing under the name Cheryl Hardy, her published non-fiction titles include *Energetic Patterns: Healing Touch Case Studies* (Vol. 1) and *Collecting Your Bones*. *Being Noah* is her first novel.

Cheryl's love of writing was a focus for most of her life. She treated writing as a creative and spiritual experience. She received a BA in Journalism from Mesa College in 1976. In 2019 Cheryl received her MFA from Western Colorado University, but she passed away shortly before graduation.

Cheryl recently worked as a certified healing touch instructor and taught a program and workshop focusing on holistic living. Cheryl has one son, two daughters, and seven grandchildren and she resided in Colorado.

This novel was written as part of her MFA program, and WordFire Press is proud to publish it for the first time.

IF YOU LIKED

BEING NOAH, YOU MIGHT ALSO ENJOY:

Keeper of the Winds
by Russell Davis

A Furnace Sealed
by Keith R.A. de Candido

Indomitable

by J.B. Garner

This book was produced as part of the Publishing MA program for Western Colorado University's Graduate Program in Creative Writing.

OTHER WORDFIRE PRESS TITLES

Into the Fire
by Patrick Hester

Crystal Doors
by Rebecca Moesta &
Kevin J. Anderson

The Magic Touch
by Jody Lynn Nye

Our list of other WordFire Press authors and titles is always growing.
To find out more and to see our selection of titles, visit us at:

wordfirepress.com